KILRONE—INDIAN FIGHTER

One Indian rode off to the far right, cutting off any hope of escape. The other four Indians came straight at him. Kilrone leapt off his horse. He stood there wide-legged and braced as the Indians swept down on him. His first shot slammed into the chest of the nearest brave. A lance ripped through Kilrone's shirt and a horse knocked him sprawling. But Kilrone came up shooting, and suddenly the afternoon was filled with the thunder of rifles.

KILRONE

**LOUIS L'AMOUR'S STIRRING SAGA
OF ONE MAN'S COURAGE
AGAINST ALL ODDS!**

Bantam Books by Louis L'Amour

Ask your bookseller for the books you have missed

KILRONE
LOUIS L'AMOUR

BANTAM BOOKS
TORONTO · NEW YORK · LONDON
NEW YORK

KILRONE
A Bantam Book | October 1966

2nd printing	August 1970	3rd printing	September 1970

New Bantam edition | September 1971

2nd printing	October 1971	8th printing	January 1975
3rd printing	June 1972	9th printing	February 1977
4th printing	November 1972	10th printing	September 1977
5th printing	November 1973	11th printing	April 1978
6th printing	August 1974	12th printing	March 1979
7th printing	September 1974	13th printing	February 1980

*Photograph of Louis L'Amour
by John Hamilton—Globe Photos, Inc.*

ISBN 0-553-13680-1

Published simultaneously in the United States and Canada

PRINTED IN THE UNITED STATES OF AMERICA

KILRONE

Chapter 1

Betty Considine shaded her eyes when she saw the rider coming through the gate. Accustomed to the movements of horses and men, she noted the weary, shuffling trot of the pony as it crossed the baked clay of the compound toward the Headquarters building.

The rider was unshaven, and the dark hair curled around his ears and over the collar of his sun-bleached shirt. When he swung down she noted the gun hung low, the narrow hips, and the powerful shoulders. His hat brim was ragged, and there was a bullet hole through the crown.

When he was a few paces from her she could clearly see the line of an old scar on his cheekbone. His lean brown face was haggard, and in his eyes there was the daze of a dreadful weariness. On the collar and shoulder of his faded blue shirt was a dark stain of dried blood.

Pulling his hat from his head, he slapped it against his thigh in an ineffectual effort to free it of dust, and the attempt caused him to stagger, so that he half fell against the hitch rail.

She ran to him and put her hand on his shoulder. "Are you hurt?" she asked quickly. "What's the matter?"

The face he turned to her was etched with lines of exhaustion, and was gray under the tan. "I'll be all right. Thank you."

He smelled strongly of stale sweat, dust, and the horse, and he gathered himself with a visible effort. Even in his exhausted state there was a faint swagger in his bearing.

"Who's commanding?" he asked.

"The adjutant, Major Paddock."

He had started to turn away, but at the name his shoulders seemed to hunch as from a blow. He looked back at her, the glaze of weariness gone from his eyes. "You said *Paddock*. Not Frank Bell Paddock?"

"Yes. Do you know him?"

He stared at the compound as if seeing it for the first time. Squinting against the white-hot glare of the desert sun, he looked around the rectangle of shabby adobes that made up the tiny post. Officers' quarters, adjutant's office, sutler's store, the post bakery, commissary, quartermaster stores, blacksmith shop, corrals, and stables.

Everywhere was heat, dust, and the glare of the pitiless sun. "My God!" he said softly. "Frank Bell Paddock!"

He opened the door of the Headquarters building and disappeared inside.

Betty Considine was Army. The only daughter of General Pat Considine, and a niece of Carter Hanlon, captain and army surgeon, she had grown up to Regulations. Having lived on a dozen army posts, after her father's death she had gone to live with her aunt and uncle. She was familiar with army gossip and she knew, as they all did, the story of Major Frank Bell Paddock.

If this stranger was shocked at the presence of Major Paddock at this remote post he must have known Paddock in the past, but not during the years immediately behind him. There had been a time when Paddock was considered one of the most promising young officers in the post-war Army, and one with an assured future.

Since that time his decline had been consistent, but the only other consistent thing about Paddock was his addiction to the bottle. Finally he had come here, only a year ago, to this new and temporary fort, one of the most isolated in the country.

Her curiosity aroused, Betty Considine paused in the shade of the overhang outside the sutler's store.

Uninterested in any man on the post or elsewhere, Betty was intrigued by this disreputable-looking stranger who had known Frank Bell Paddock in the days of his glory.

If this man had known Paddock, he must have known him back east, or in Europe, yet a more typical western

man she had never seen. But he might have been Army
. . . even if he did not look it now.

The life of Major Frank Bell Paddock was an open
book up to a point, but Something had happened in
Paris.

Captain Paddock had been a military attaché at the
American embassy in Paris, a handsome, athletic young
officer, admired by his superiors. There he had met and
married Denise de Caslou, a famous beauty, of the old
nobility. She came of a family of little wealth but one
known for the long line of soldiers and men of the sea,
men of bravery and distinction.

Whatever it was that happened had occurred only a
year after their marriage, and with it began the decline
and fall of Frank Bell Paddock.

Suddenly relieved of duty in Paris, he had been returned to the States, and after several brief stays at
various posts, he was sent to a remote fort in Dakota,
and then to Montana.

Now, at the end of the long road down, Major Frank
Bell Paddock was adjutant of a post with only four
troops of cavalry, all of them under strength. Always
mildly under the influence of alcohol, he was never
trusted with a field command. Promotion was something
for which he could no longer hope, and he was merely
living out the years until he could retire on a pension.
But those years stretched far ahead for Paddock, who
was not yet forty.

This was the man Barney Kilrone faced as he stepped
past the company clerk and into the office beyond. The
once fine features of the officer he remembered had
coarsened into heaviness, and there was a premature
graying. Most of all, there was an air of resignation, of
hopelessness about the man. When Paddock looked up,
his expression hardened into anger as he recognized
Kilrone.

"So—" It was almost a sigh. "It is you again."

"On business, Pad, very ugly business. I Troop is gone
. . . wiped out. The Bannocks hit them from ambush
over on the Little Owyhee."

Major Paddock dropped his eyes to the now mean
ingless papers on the desk. Nineteen men ... and th
prisoners, if any, worse off than the dead. If any ha
gotten away they were now being hunted down like ra
in a cornfield.

"Colonel Webb?"

"I wouldn't know him by sight, Pad, and identificatio
would have been impossible anyway."

Paddock's brain, dulled by whiskey and long hours c
paper work, refused to fit himself into the new picture
Something must be done. . . .

There were two problems here, one military and th
other personal. The man who had wrecked his life wa
facing him now, his very presence proof that the year
of expectancy had not been in vain. He had come at last
and when he left he would take with him all worthwhil
in life that remained to the dashing young officer tha
had been Frank Bell Paddock.

"You've come for Denise?"

"Don't be a fool, Pad! Impatience drove through hi
exhaustion. "She loves you. She always did. She's you
wife."

"She has been loyal, I grant you, Barney. She has bee
... what is it the French say? Correct? But she's been i
love with you."

He sat back in his chair. "She's more beautiful tha
ever, Barney; and now you've come to take her away, a
I knew you would."

"Pad, for God's sake, forget it! I didn't even know yo
were in this part of the country until a girl outside tol
me just now. I've been moving, Pad. I haven't thought o
Denise in years, and I am sure she hasn't thought of me."

The minutes ticked by; a fly buzzed against the win
dow, struggling to escape the heavy air of the hot, clos
room. It was Barnes Kilrone who broke the silence
"Pad, you're in command. This is your problem ... all o
it."

"Command?" The word carried a shock that penetrat
ed Paddock's cocoon of self-pity.

Command? What did one do with three troops? Three? ...

"My God!" He came to his feet, his face drawn and bloodless. "M Troop ... they were to rendezvous with I Troop on the North Fork!"

Barney Kilrone held himself up by the edge of the desk, and his brain struggled against fatigue, for he was all in. He thought of M Troop riding across country, a tired lot of men, riding to a meeting with a company of the vanquished, a company of the dead ... and who would keep that rendezvous?

The Bannocks!

Discipline, the habit of soldiering, began to shape its pattern in the mind of Major Frank Paddock. His thoughts began to take formation. He had no plan, of course, to meet this eventuality, but he knew the things to be considered, the responsibilities that were his. M Troop must be warned ... somehow.

Two troops remained on the post, two troops comprising just seventy-two effectives, and the whole Bannock operation might be directed toward a piecemeal destruction of the garrison at the post. The Bannocks, led by a shrewd and careful fighter, had ambushed I Troop before they could effect the meeting with M Troop.

With the first troop destroyed, Medicine Dog could now move to ambush the second. If he was aware the post had been warned he would expect a relief force to come ... and trust him to know just how many soldiers remained of the post complement, and how many could be spared to leave the fort. And how pitifully few would remain.

"It's the post he wants," Paddock said aloud. "He wants the ammunition, the guns, the food, and the horses. If he could draw enough of us away from the post he could strike here. . . ."

He broke off, and his eyes turned to Kilrone. "Barney, how did you get here? Were you seen?"

"If I'd been seen I wouldn't be here. Unless they return to the scene of the fight and see my tracks around, they can't know."

"Unless they let you come on purpose to draw another troop away from the post." He sank back into his chair.

It was time for a decision, and Frank Paddock had no decision. He needed time ... time. Everything would depend on what he decided. If the troop he sent to the relief of M Troop was caught before it could effect a meeting and was itself destroyed, then the post would be helpless before such an attack as the Bannocks could mount.

For the first time he became aware of the condition of the man across the desk. At once he was on his feet. "Come on, Barney—you're all in. Come to my quarters."

Kilrone held back. "Take me to the barracks. To the stables . . . not to your quarters."

"Now you're being the fool." Paddock took Kilrone's arm. In a way, he thought, it would be better to have it over. After all the years of waiting it would be a relief.

Betty Considine saw them come out the door, and she came up quickly. "Major Paddock, can I be of help?"

A fourth person might make it easier. . . . "All right," he said. "Glad to have you. I know he needs rest, and he seems to have been wounded."

At Paddock's quarters, it was Betty who opened the door, and she saw the expression on Denise Paddock's face when she glimpsed the stranger. She seemed to stiffen, then pale, but she was at once composed. "This way," she said.

She led the way to the spare bedroom and helped her husband draw off the brush-scratched, desert-worn boots. It was she who noted the blood-stained collar and located the wound. Betty, looking past Denise, saw the dressing on the wound. "He escaped from the Indians?" she asked.

Kilrone, who had kept on his feet until they entered the room, had collapsed at the bedside and now lay on the bed unconscious.

"Why do you ask that?"

"That's an Indian dressing. I've seen them before."

Paddock looked down at the man on the bed. No, he was not really unconscious, merely sleeping heavily. An

Indian had dressed that wound ... and he had denied being seen by the Bannocks.

Denise had removed the dressing, and Paddock stared at the puckering wound. "That's not fresh," he said.

"Three days," Betty guessed. "Maybe four." She had helped her uncle treat too many injured men in these past few years not to know.

An Indian dressing on a wound, and no friendly Indian within miles. A wound several days old, and he had come from the heart of Indian country.

Suppose—one had to suppose everything—suppose the man was a renegade? What better way to scatter the forces of a post and leave it helpless?

Paddock told himself he must forget all he had known of Captain Barnes Kilrone in the past. Nor must he think now of Denise. There was too little time. He had a decision to make.

Captain Mellett and the forty-seven men of M Troop would reach the North Fork by sundown tomorrow. It was doubtful if the Bannocks would attack before daylight the following morning. There was always the possibility that some survivor of the massacre of I Troop would get through to Mellett with a warning, but that was an outside chance. Mellett was a seasoned officer, sure to be careful, but even the best of men could be trapped.

Every minute of delay put Mellet closer to probable death by ambuscade. Between Mellett's troop and possible massacre stood only the judgment of Major Frank Paddock. And to send out a troop to relieve Mellett would leave the post vulnerable to attack, practically helpless.

His decision had to rest on the word of one man—a man who perhaps could not be trusted ... or could he?

Paddock stepped out into the heat and dust of the compound and closed the door behind him. If he could get another troop into position to hit the Bannocks as they attacked Mellett, he would have them between two fires and might wipe them out. It was a challenging thought. This could be enough to erase all his past failures.

But it involved a problem almost too difficult for him to come to grips with—a problem full of uncertainties. Could he get K Troop in position in time to help Mellett? Dare he accept the risk of leaving the post exposed to attack? Suppose the Bannocks had already foreseen that possibility, and even now might have the bulk of their men ready for an attack on the post and its few remaining soldiers? ... Or K Troop might fail to reach Mellett in time, and be trapped themselves.

He went back to his desk and stared at the map on the wall. It was ninety miles to the North Fork, and K Troop would have no more than thirty-six hours in which to cover the distance, all of it rough, dangerous country where the enemy might be encountered at any moment.

His thoughts returned to the man who was the source of his information.

What was Captain Barney Kilrone, once considered the most dashing and romantic officer in the Army, doing in Nevada, looking and acting like a renegade?

He, Frank Bell Paddock, had changed, and he knew why; but what had happened to Barney Kilrone?

Chapter 2

From his desk Paddock could look out of three windows, each offering a different view, and he liked none of them.

From one window he could see the mountains, their lower slopes bare of trees. They were beautiful in their aloof loneliness, but he had no feeling for their beauty, nor for the sweep of plain he saw from the window on the other side—flat, open country stretching to the horizon. Straight before him was a window beside the door that led to the outer office, and from this window he could look out on the parade ground, and could see the doors of the buildings along either side.

Thus, from his desk he could see everyone who moved out there, including those who came and went from his own house, and they were not many. He detested this bleak and lonely post, and he was positive that Denise felt as he did.

She, who had been the center of attention in Paris and Vienna, had only two friends here: Betty Considine, of course, and Stella Rybolt, wife of Lieutenant August Rybolt. There was, he admitted reluctantly, one other friend Denise had, one of whom he disapproved.

Mary Tall Singer was an Indian girl, a Shoshone who had acquired an education when as a child she had attracted the attention of yet another lonely Army wife. For lack of something else to do, the Colonel's wife had taken the pretty Indian girl into her home, taught her to read, write, and sew, to conduct herself as a lady, and to appreciate literature. By one means or another Mary had acquired books and had read them—from children's books, easily read, she had before long moved on to the better novels, and to history and poetry.

She now worked as a clerk, assisting the sutler. He was a sober, serious man who had profited by her advice in his dealings with the Indians, and who respected her intelligence and paid her as much as he would have paid a man doing the same job.

Her status at the post was peculiar. Despite the fact that she was an Indian, single and very pretty, she was treated as a white woman in the same position might have been treated. That this was so was due not only to her position in the sutler's eyes, but to the fact, well known, that she was a friend of Denise Paddock.

Frank Bell Paddock continued to stare gloomily out of the window. He was thinking that Denise had succeeded where he had failed, for at this lonely outpost she had created a world of her own in which she held her position calmly and with assurance. The senior officer at the post was a bachelor, hence Denise had become official hostess at whatever social events were possible.

The fact that she was resented by the other officers' wives on the post disturbed her not in the least, nor did the fact that they tried to look down on her because of her friendship with Mary Tall Singer.

In Stella Rybolt and Betty Considine she had friends who felt as she did about Mary as well as about much else. Stella Rybolt was a veteran of half a dozen army posts, and she knew all the tricks of making do. Long ago she had accepted the fact that her husband would never be more than a company commander, and she was unconcerned about it. Gus Rybolt was a good, steady man who loved his wife and his duty; he held to regulations, but knew when to look the other way when others did not, just as long as it did not affect the morale of his own men or the safety of the post.

Stella Rybolt had lived twenty-eight of her forty-five years on army posts, most of them on the frontier. She knew the regulations and accepted them as a fact of life, just the same as the rising and the setting of the sun; hence she had no quarrel with the army. She loved the West and its people, but had looked warily at first on Denise Paddock. Knowing Denise's background, she had half expected her to be a snob. But the first day Denise had smiled, held out her hand, and said, "Mrs. Rybolt, I am new to this post. Don't let me make any mistakes."

The following morning the coffee sessions had begun, the first at Stella Rybolt's, the second at Dr. Hanlon's; and by the third day Denise was sufficiently settled to have them at her quarters, and the others were envious of the grace and beauty she had given them.

Denise had made the best of each situation as it came, and never was there a word of complaint from her.

Frank Paddock gnawed now at his mustache. He had never liked this country, and one of the reasons he had not liked it was because it symbolized his defeat.

Nobody had started better than he. Nobody was given a better chance to succeed. The year he graduated the betting was that he would be the first in his class to make general, and no takers. Yet here he was, at an almost forgotten post, an almost forgotten man.

But now there was a chance, the first chance in a long time, the last chance he might ever have. If he could ride out there and trap the Bannocks, if he could score a smashing defeat . . .

It was all he would need. He had a friend, a newspaperman who was now traveling in the West, and he was a man to make much of such a story.

There might be a promotion, there might be a recall to some eastern post. He well knew what an opportunity like that could do for a man. And the chance was here.

At this moment he wanted a drink badly. The bottle was there, nearly full, in his bottom drawer, within reach of his hand. Yet he did not reach for it.

Ambitious he might be, but he was still a soldier, and he was in command. Whatever he did must be done with the utmost skill; and he must take no chance that he could not later explain.

I Troop was gone, Colonel Webb was dead. These things he accepted as fact. Kilrone might be a renegade,

but he was not willing to believe it. Nonetheless, it was
a thought he must keep in mind.

Mellett would be going into bivouac by now. Trust
Mellett to choose his spot well, to select a good defensive position, and to scout the country around while it
was still light.

The Bannocks would not attack while he was in position, for they knew what kind of a soldier Mellett was.
They would try to catch him on the move, preferably
near the point of rendezvous, and until that moment
they would keep out of sight. So Paddock had a little
time.

He already knew that he would lead the relief force
himself. His opportunity lay in victory in the field, not
from a desk.

Desperately, he wished for Gus Rybolt. If Rybolt
were only here he could leave him in command at the
post. He was tough, dependable, every inch a soldier.
But Lieutenant Rybolt had gone to Halleck with a guard
of six men to escort the pay wagon, and he was not due
back for three days. By that time the emergency would
have passed, and all would be settled, one way or the
other . . .

Paddock knew that for a victory, a really decisive
victory, he would need every man he could get. He
made up his mind then to strip the post. A man had to
gamble, and he was going to gamble that the Bannocks
wanted to take Mellett and M Troop, and that they
would not attempt an attack on the post. Carefully he
avoided thinking of the alternative. He even avoided
thinking of Denise, except to think that he was doing
this for her.

In the back of his mind was the thought that success
meant the East, an easier life, a good post, perhaps even
Washington, D.C., where a wife such as Denise would
be a tremendous asset. It meant escape from all he had
become, a return to all he had been.

Betty Considine got up from the table and tiptoed to
the door of the bedroom. Kilrone was asleep, so she

eased quietly into the room and over to his bed, and looked down at the exhausted man.

He was strikingly good-looking, with an almost saturnine cast of countenance. Lying on the bed, he looked uncommonly long and lean, but his shoulders were broad. She had noticed when checking the bullet wound, that his body carried half a dozen scars of blade or bullet ... and at least one that looked like an arrow wound.

"He is handsome, isn't he?" Denise said.

Betty turned to glance at Denise. "Yes ... yes, he is," she said. Then she added, "I wonder why he's up here? This is so out of the way."

"Not for him. That's Barnes Kilrone."

Seeing that the name meant nothing to Betty, Denise went on, "Seven years or so ago, all you had to do was mention his name and you would hear a dozen Kilrone stories, all different."

"You knew him?"

"It's a long story and a painful one." Denise turned toward the kitchen. "I'll make some coffee."

She took down the can from the shelf. "Were you there when he talked to Frank?" she asked.

"No."

Denise measured the coffee, making no further comment, but Betty was curious. "What is he like?"

"Barney? To most women he was the soul of romance. He always had a touch of the dramatic about him. Wherever he was, things happened, and usually they happened to *him*. I think many of the men were envious of him."

"Jealous?"

Denise paused, giving Betty a cool, thoughtful look, as if wondering if Betty was prying. "Some of them, at least," she said finally; "although usually with less reason than they believed.

"He was twenty-five then," she went on, "and seemed older. He had seen a bit more and done a bit more than any of the others we knew. I expect half the women who knew him were in love with him at one time or another. When we first met everyone was talking about him. He had been in Paris less than a week and had already fought a duel with a French newspaperman over some comments about a dancer Barney liked."

"A duel? You mean a real duel?"

"Barney wanted sabers, but as the challenged party the Frenchman chose rapiers. He believed that no American would be familiar with them. He couldn't have been more mistaken—Barney was a fine swordsman. The newspaperman went to the hospital and Barney became a celebrity."

Denise stopped and looked up, listening. She knew Frank's step, and Betty knew what she was listening for. She had seen Denise listening just like this many times before. But when he came in he was cold sober, and his eyes held an odd glint of resolution, an unfamiliar light in the eyes of Frank Paddock.

For the first time, then, the two women learned what had happened. He gave it to them briefly, concisely. "Denise, I Troop is gone . . . massacred. Colonel Webb is dead."

They stared at him, unable to grasp the enormity of it. Tragedy was familiar to them. Both had been on other posts in Indian fighting country, each knew how quickly death could strike. But a whole troop . . . and Colonel Webb!

"I am in command." There was a hard ring to his voice, a ring Betty had never heard, and one that Denise had heard rarely. "I am taking K Troop out in the morning."

He sat down and explained the situation as it concerned Captain Mellett. He must be warned; and if K Troop arrived in time they might also catch the Bannocks unaware and overcome them once and for all. He would be leaving before daylight.

He said nothing of his fears that the fort itself might be attacked. Carefully, he shunted away all thought of the stores of rifles, ammunition, and food that had been laid in at the fort against a fall campaign. It was likely the Bannocks knew of those stores, and he was not sure they did not have information from within the fort itself. But he counted on a quick, decisive victory that would preclude all possibility of an attack on the fort. Besides, he would leave a token force. He avoided thinking of how inadequate that force would be if he reinforced K Troop as he planned.

Betty was appalled at the thought of I Troop gone. She knew them all, every man-jack of them, as her uncle would say. Captain Tom Whitman had been a whist-playing friend of her uncle, and was often in the house. Sergeant Bill Jordan had taught her to ride when he was a private working on his first enlistment. Hauffer was a stern, quiet man who had been an officer in the Prussian army. Nobody knew or inquired how he happened to come to the western frontier ... such questions simply were not asked.

Lister had tired of trying to make it on a government claim in Kansas ... Ryan had recently arrived from Ireland ... Johnson, whose name had been something else back in the States ... and Spinarski, a sullen Slav who talked only to the horses, with whom he was on the best of terms.

All gone ... massacred!

Captain Mellett would soon be going into bivouac ... M Troop's last bivouac? Tomorrow they would ride to their rendezvous with destiny at North Fork.

Betty knew the place. She had been there once on a picnic in more peaceful times than these—a lonely, lovely place of wild, rugged beauty. To a soldier, in such a time of Indian trouble as this, it might be a death trap.

M Troop mustered forty-seven men, and at least twenty were hardened veterans, three of whom had been with Crook on the Rosebud; two had fought against Cochise in Arizona. Four had served enlistments in the battle-scarred Fifth Cavalry. Only six were raw recruits, and there was some suspicion that one of those had served previously and deserted ... nobody asked that question, either.

Mellett himself was a stern, tough officer. He had fought through the Civil War, advancing to colonel, and had come west to fight Indians when the war was over, accepting the reduced rank, as so many others had. All told, he had twenty years of the hardest kind of service behind him, and looked it.

Denise brought coffee for them. "I'd like to know where Kilrone picked up that bullet," Paddock said, "and who treated him for it."

"He may have friends among the Indians, Frank. You know how he was ... he always had friends in odd places."

Paddock tasted his coffee. If he did as he planned, he was thinking, who would be left behind? The sutler, who was fifty-five and fat; two farriers, who were good enough at shoeing horses and good as veterinarians if nothing serious occurred; one line sergeant on the sick list, and four teamsters. There were several cooks, and three men in the guardhouse who could, if necessary, be freed to fight.

At best, fifteen men ... not nearly enough if there was an attack.

The fort, like most western forts, was not really a fort at all. It was a group of buildings around a parade ground, with gaps between the buildings. He had never given any thought to how the place might be defended, for it had never seemed that he would have this problem. Usually there were men enough so that no force of Indians would be likely to take the risk. And he was not going to think of that now.

Coolly, even coldly, he pushed the idea aside. It simply could not be ... it must not be. The Bannocks would be concentrating on Mellett's troop, and Paddock would close in with his troop. He wanted the Indians to become thoroughly involved before he attacked; then his victory would be all the more decisive.

All the troops were far under strength. There had seemed little prospect of any serious trouble, so there had been delay in bringing them up to strength. Theoretically a troop consisted of seventy-eight men, but few had as many as that. K Troop as well as M Troop consisted of forty-seven men. With others Paddock could muster, he could bring it up to sixty.

He thought of the many letters Webb had written requesting additional men. Despite the fact that literacy and citizenship requirements were nonexistent, recruiting lagged. At that, almost half their force was of foreign extraction, the largest portion being Irish. Fortunately these made excellent soldiers and superb fighting men.

Whom to leave in command? Certainly not Pryor. Lieutenant Eden Pryor had courage enough, but he lacked both judgment and experience. Moreover, he despised the Indian as a fighting man, and was eager for a fight to prove his point. Whatever action took place here must be defensive only.

His thoughts returned to Barnes Kilrone. How did he come to be here? What was he doing out here at the shaggy end of nowhere? And what had happened to his army career?

Chapter 3

The eyes of Barnes Kilrone opened on a shadowed room, lighted by a kerosene lamp, screened to keep the light from waking him. He lay still for a time, just listening, as was his habit. It was a practice developed long ago, the practice of a man who traveled much in wild country.

His mind was immediately alert, remembering how he had come here, and remembering his exhaustion. Even now he did not wish to move, although he knew he must. There was something here that remained undone.

He had reported to the commanding officer—Frank Paddock, of all people—giving him the news of the fate of I Troop and of the officer commanding the post. Which left Major Frank Bell Paddock in command.

His eyes were on the island of light on the ceiling over the lamp, which had its wick turned low. Beyond the screen he heard a faint rustle of movement, and realized somebody was there, waiting, watching over him.

Well, he did not need care—his wound was almost healed. It was the weakness it had left him with, and the driving hard ride that had made him fold up.

Paddock ... how the man had changed! All the edge was gone. His face was puffy, and he had looked beaten. It was hell, what a man could do to himself ... for he had done it to himself—and to Denise.

Kilrone started to sit up and the bed creaked under him. Instantly there was quick movement beyond the screen, and as he sank back a girl came around it to look down at him. It was the girl he had seen outside when he first rode in.

"What's happened?" he asked her.

18

"Nothing ... yet. The command is moving out in the morning."

"Paddock? You mean he's moving to join Mellett? He mustn't."

He started up again and swung his feet to the floor. "I've got to get up."

"Why? Why mustn't he?"

He seemed about to speak, but hesitated. There was no reason to frighten them. He would talk to Paddock.

Despite Betty Considine's protests, he dressed and went to the kitchen. He looked across the room at Denise. She was as beautiful as ever, a little older, with a little less gaiety and laughter, but poised and lovely as always.

"I've got to see Frank," he said.

"Have some coffee first. You're in no condition to be walking around."

He glanced at the clock. It was nearly midnight, but the post was awake. Men were preparing their equipment to move out at dawn, or earlier. He accepted the coffee, trying to plan what he would say. After all, he was a civilian and Paddock was in command here.

Paddock heard him speak to the sergeant, and he came out of his office. He was looking better. His face even seemed to have lost its flabbiness.

"Frank, are you planning on going after them?" Kilrone asked.

"We will have them boxed," was the answer. "We can come in from south when they attack Mellett."

"What about the post?"

"No need to worry. They will be so busy with us they won't have the time to consider attacking here."

Barney Kilrone spoke quietly. "Don't do it, Frank. It's the post they're after. There were at least two hundred warriors in the lot that hit I Troop, and there are a lot of Paiutes coming up from the south. My guess would be there are at least a thousand warriors on the move right now, and even that may be too low."

"A thousand! Barney, you're daffy. The Bannocks could never muster that many, even with the Paiutes."

"Frank, believe me, they've got them."

Paddock turned away. He did not wish to listen to such talk, nor did he want to have the feeling of guilt that rose within him. He knew he was taking a risk, but he refused to admit it, even to himself. If he sat tight, if he failed to move now, there would be no point to anything.

He might stay right here, and no one could object to his sitting still and taking care of the post, guarding it against possible attack. But the alternative was a possible victory for him, with headlines in the news and, as soon as it could be managed, recall to an eastern post. That was what he must keep in mind.

"Mellett must be given help," he said stubbornly. "We have a chance to crush this outbreak once and for all. I shall move to join him at the moment of attack." He looked around at Kilrone. "You're welcome to ride along, if you feel up to it."

"I'll stay here," Kilrone said quietly.

Paddock glanced at him, his eyes suddenly cold. "You do that," he said. And then he added, "Will you be here when I get back? Or will you choose this opportunity to take Denise away?"

Anger exploded in Kilrone. "Damn it, Frank, Denise has a mind of her own! Nobody can *take* her anywhere! I told you before, she is in love with you. She has always been."

He turned away and went outside. The night was cold, warning of what was to come. Kilrone stood watching the bustle of activity ... undoubtedly there was an Indian somewhere not far away who was also watching, pleased with what he saw. And that Indian would be riding soon, to carry the news.

Kilrone knew he was an outsider here, practically an interloper. He no longer belonged to the Army, no longer had anything to do with this. Yet it was in him, the memory of it, the feel of it, the smells of stables, of leather, of gunsmoke. Soberly, he watched the subdued haste, the lights in the windows, knowing that hurried good-byes were being said, the women smiling bravely to hide their fears, the men being roughly casual about it all, hiding their own worries, which were rarely for themselves but rather for what would happen to their families if they did not come back.

He had been through this at Camp Date Creek, at Fort Riley, at half a dozen other posts. Not that he had ever left anyone behind . . . and that was the worst of it. Some of the men here tonight would be leaving no one behind. He knew how that felt. You sat in your saddle while the women said good-bye, clung to their husbands for that last moment, reluctant to let them go. You sat straight, looking right across your horse's ears and you knew nobody really gave a damn if you came back or not . . . unless it was the sergeant who kept the duty roster.

It was going to be rough out there. If Paddock was thinking of anything at all except a quick, crushing victory, he was thinking of Egan or Buffalo Horn. Well, it would be neither of them. Egan was a peace-loving Indian who did not really want to fight; and Buffalo Horn had his head full of the reputation Chief Joseph had made, and wanted to beat it.

Anyway, Buffalo Horn was busy up in Oregon, and this action was the inspiration of Medicine Dog, and you had to live close to the Indians to understand about Medicine Dog.

Kilrone saw the lone horseman riding toward him, coming up through the shadows from the stables, a man who did not ride like a cavalryman. The rider drew up a dozen feet off and deliberately lit a cigarette to let Kilrone see his face.

It was a long, horse face with a drooping mustache, and the man was a civilian in nondescript dress. The horse was a good one, a mustang, but long-legged and solidly built.

"Howdy," the man said. "Seen you ride in. You're Kilrone, ain't you? Seen you one time down to Cheyenne."

"Who are you?"

"I'm Ben Hayes. Scoutin' for this outfit."

"I came in from the southeast," Kilrone offered. "You've got trouble coming."

"I told him."

"You know who they've got with them down there?" Kilrone took a cigar from his shirt pocket. "Medicine Dog," he said.

Hayes stared. "You're sure?"

"A short, stocky Indian with bandy legs, a deep scar through his upper lip."

"That's him." Hayes swore slowly, viciously. "He's mean . . . pizen mean. And smart, real smart."

"Tell Paddock, will you? I tried."

Ben Hayes was silent. After a moment he said, "The more I think on it the more I wonder. Medicine Dog would like to get Mellett . . . be a big feather for him."

Barney Kilrone spoke abruptly. "Medicine Dog is a realist, Hayes. Mellett would be an important scalp for any Indian. But Medicine Dog doesn't want a scalp—he wants the food, the horses, most of all the ammunition.

"Think, man," he went on. "If the Dog takes this camp, where can Mellett go? He's riding about a hundred rounds to the man. He'll have a fight up on North Fork and he'll use some of it . . . say half if it goes as I believe it will. The Dog will have this camp. He'll have guns, plenty of ammunition, food. He'll have some uniforms, too."

"What's that mean?"

"The Dog is only half Bannock, remember. The other half is Sioux. As a boy back in Dakota he dressed in a uniform, along with a couple dozen others, to trap and kill some scouts who thought they were joining an Army command. Using the same trick, he led a party into a stage station down Wyoming way. I think he'd try it again."

"I'll talk to the Major." Hayes sounded doubtful. "I got no use for a desk soldier," he added.

"Don't take this one lightly, Hayes. I know him. He was one of the best troop commanders I ever knew when he was younger."

For several minutes neither man spoke, each busy

with his own thoughts. The parade ground was beginning to empty, and a few lights had gone out. There was time for a couple of hours of sleep before the column moved out. With no place to go, Kilrone knew he would return to Paddock's quarters, and he would be expected there. Yet he felt a curious reluctance to return, although if that girl was there ... what was her name?

He turned his thoughts to her seriously for the first time. She was pretty—beautiful in her own special way—but it was her quiet competence that had impressed him. He had a vague recollection of her examining his wound.

"Hayes," he said suddenly, "I'm new at this post. If a man had to leave here, with a party of women and children, is there any place he could go? Some place in the hills, I mean? A place a man could defend?"

"You'd need time. You ain't a-goin' to have it." Hayes looked straight at him. "You stayin' here?"

"They'll need me."

"Good luck."

Ben Hayes rode across the grounds toward the stables. He would be catching some sleep himself.

"Mr. Kilrone?" he turned his head and saw Betty Considine standing beside him. "You should be resting. You're suffering from exhaustion and from the results of your wound."

"And you?"

"I am tired." She spoke quietly, with no plea for sympathy. "It has been a long day."

He started back toward Paddock's quarters, keeping pace with her. "I often wonder who chooses the locations for these posts," he commented. "They are always in the hottest, driest, windiest, or coldest places."

"I heard you tell Ben you were staying."

"Well, you said I need rest. This is as good a place as any for that. I always swore when I left the Army I'd find a place near an army post where reveille would wake me up ... and then I'd turn over and go to sleep again."

She laughed. "And did you?"

"No. I found that I missed the Army too much. There's always the temptation to go back, you know, because it's safe."

"Safe?" She sounded incredulous.

"Of course. If you're an enlisted man your decisions are all made for you. If you're an officer there's the regulations, and the fact that everything has to go through channels. If things go wrong or you make a mistake, you can always find somebody else to blame. You don't have to worry about where you will eat or sleep, or how you'll pay medical bills, and the margins within which you can operate, so far as behavior is concerned, are well laid out."

"So why did you leave the service? Or have you?"

"Oh, I left it, all right! A situation developed with an Indian agent of whom I didn't approve, but it seemed it was not my business to approve or disapprove, so I went to work and gathered evidence. I built a very careful case, affidavits, physical evidence ... everything.

"My commanding officer warned me that the Indian agent was a personal friend of a very important man in the War Department, and if I persisted my career was very likely at an end."

"You persisted?"

"Yes."

"What happened?"

"My carefully built case was lost somewhere in transit, and I was given the word that promotions would be nonexistent for me ... at least until there was a change of administration."

"You resigned?"

"Yes ... and then I went to see the Indian agent. We discussed the situation, and then he resigned, too. And left for a healthier climate."

They stood outside the door. "And then?"

"I went down into Mexico looking for a lost gold mine, rode as a shotgun messenger for a stage company, ramrodded a cattle drive, staked a mining claim in Colorado until I was starved out, fought through a revolution in Central America, went east guarding a gold shipment."

"And now?"

"Drifting . . . looking for a place to light."

She was disappointed, although what difference it could make to her she did not know. It seemed a pointless existence. Of course, many men were doing just what Kilrone was doing, but for him it seemed wrong. He had been a young officer with a future.

They still stood there outside Paddock's quarters. "You're staying with Mrs. Paddock?" he asked.

"Only tonight. I live over there." She indicated a house two doors away. "Dr. Hanlon is my uncle. He is the post surgeon."

"Carter Hanlon? Wasn't he stationed at Fort Concho for a while?"

"Yes. Did you know him?"

"He plugged up a couple of holes for me, one time. He's a good man."

He looked at her thoughtfully, and then said, "She's a wonderful person, Denise Paddock is. She left a lot for him."

"I don't think she has ever been sorry," Betty said. "Sorry for him, I think, but not for herself. She has a rare quality of making a home wherever she is, and of finding the beautiful in every place."

She kept her eyes on his. "That was an Indian dressing on your wound," she said.

He was amused. "I'm not a renegade or a squaw man, if that is what you are thinking."

In the light from the open door he could see that she flushed. "I was thinking nothing of the kind."

Denise came to the door. "Unless you want to sleep, come into the kitchen. Frank has gone to bed."

Barney Kilrone dropped into a chair. He was tired, dead-tired, but he did not feel like sleeping. And there was something he needed to know.

"Have there been many Indians around the post in the past few weeks?" he asked.

"No," Betty said, "none at all. In fact, Ben Hayes has

been going around muttering because of it. He always says when you see no Indians, look out."

"Why do you ask?" Denise said.

"Because Medicine Dog knows everything about this post. He knows how many men are fit for service, he knows about the store of ammunition and supplies, he knows about the extra horses. Within a short time after Major Paddock rides out with his command, he will know that too."

They were both looking at him now. "Do you mean there is somebody here, somebody on this post, who is giving him information?" Betty was incredulous.

"That's hard to believe," Denise said.

"It always is," Kilrone said dryly. "That's why it's so easy. Nobody is ever willing to suspect someone they know, someone who sits down at the table with them. But a traitor can be anybody."

"Not anybody," Denise protested.

"The fact remains that everything is known. I must talk to Frank again, Denise, or you must. He has to realize that."

"What would you have him do?"

"Try and get a messenger to Mellett, recalling him. Meanwhile, ride out from the post as he plans, but go only a few miles, then return and go into hiding near here."

"What about Captain Mellett?"

"The man's an experienced Indian fighter, and I know that unless he is surprised he can fight off any Indian attack he is apt to meet. The real attack will come here, at the post."

"Frank doesn't think so," Denise said.

Barney Kilrone was silent. An attack by Paddock at the critical moment could well be decisive. And it would read well in dispatches, while a defensive action against Indians, no matter if successful, would be dismissed without comment either by his superiors or by the press. Major Frank Bell Paddock, who might never have another such chance, was going to take this one.

Only the lives to be risked were those at the post—the men, women, and children who would be left behind, unprotected.

Chapter 4

Captain Charles Mellett, who knew the challenge of command, rode up the low hill in the late afternoon and halted his troop where the land fell away on all sides. Just below the hill's highest point there was a sandy hollow. No doubt the buffalo had begun it, rolling in the sand to rid themselves of ticks or fleas, but the wind had scoured the hollow, making it wider and deeper.

Just over the highest rise of the hill there was a staggered cluster of junipers that formed a windbreak, as well as a screen for the camp's activity. On the south side, runoff water had cut a small ravine that joined a larger one at the base of the hill. Where the two joined there was a cluster of huge old cottonwoods. The stream itself was a few inches deep, a few feet wide. The water was clear and quite cold.

Mellett turned in his saddle to speak to Dunivant. "Sergeant, water your stock. Let them graze for one hour, then take them to water again. After that, put your picket line close in. Establish the guard posts at once."

Again he checked the country around. There was a good field of fire on three sides and, except for the small ravine, no available cover for at least a hundred yards in that direction.

"Corporal Hessler," he directed, "when the horses have been watered for the second time, I want that brush dumped into the ravine. Arrange it so that we cannot be approached up that ravine without a disturbance being created."

Dr. Hanlon dismounted. "You're expecting a fight?"

"This is Indian country," Mellett replied. "I always expect a fight."

The men of M Troop, who knew their commander,

were already busy shaping the camp into a crude but effective temporary fort, dragging a fallen log into position here, throwing up a modest breastwork there.

Mellett's rules were few but definite. Every camp a defensive position, all cookfires out before twilight, all horses picketed close in by sundown, each camp chosen not so much for their own comfort as to deprive an enemy of cover or concealment.

Captain Mellett had fought the Sioux and the Cheyenne, the Arapaho, Kiowa, and Comanche, the Nez Percé, and the Apache, and he knew what an Indian was like. The Indian he knew was a wily and dangerous warrior, a first-class fighting man who had his own set of rules and his own ideas of bravery.

As the camp was settling down for the night, Dr. Hanlon commented over coffee, "We've seen no Indians."

Mellett took out a cigar and lit it. "I never like to argue with my superiors, and Webb knows this business as well as I do, but at a time like this, with Buffalo Horn out, I think he had too small a force for a patrol."

"You think he's in trouble?"

"I doubt it, but it's taking a chance, Cart. You know that yourself. Oh, I'm not particularly worried about Buffalo Horn. The last we heard, he's away up north and west from here ... he's Harney's problem. But there's something else in the wind, and I don't like the smell of it.

"Jim Webb knew that when he was sent up here from Halleck. We've had no burned ranches, no settlers killed in this area, though there's been a lot of it over west. That argues that somebody is keeping them from it, and the question is—why?"

"They may be taking a spoke from Washakie's wheel. He's avoided any sign of trouble with the whites."

"I know. This is something else, because those Indians south and east of here have turned mean. Mean, but quiet, and that's not their way. Webb's theory is that somebody who carries a lot of weight with them is holding them back for something really big."

"What, do you suppose?"

"I don't know." Mellett looked at his cigar tip. "Just the same, I'm glad that K Troop is back there at the post with Paddock."

"A drunk."

"Basically a good soldier, Cart. He's been drinking, I'll allow, but the man knows the way of things, and when the chips are down, he knows what to do."

"Did you know Kilrone?"

"Served with him. He never went by the book, but he was good. Maybe the best I ever served with, unless it was Paddock himself.

"We used to talk about Indians, and believe me, nobody ever knew them better than Kilrone. He said something once that I've never forgotten. We'd been talking about the way the Mongols banded together under one man after all their tribal wars, and swept over most of Asia and part of Europe.

"Kilrone commented, 'You can just thank the Good Lord that the Indian never developed such a man.' His theory was that the only thing that saved us from being swept away was the fact that the tribal thinking of the Indian kept them from uniting.

"Suppose Tecumseh—and he had the idea—had been able to weld the tribes together under some such leader as Crazy Horse or Chief Joseph? We've never whipped a well-armed Indian force, you know. They never had as many rifles as they needed, and never enough ammunition, and fortunately for us the Indian's idea of war was based on a one-battle, one-war tradition. Joseph had arrived at the idea of the campaign, but he was fighting a rear-guard action with only some three hundred-odd fighting men, and all his women and children along."

"I'd never thought of it that way."

"We've been lucky, Cart. Genghis Khan found the Mongols split up, living a life not too different from that of the Indians, and busy with tribal warfare and tribal hatreds. He brought them all together, and look what happened."

"You don't think anything like that is developing now, surely?"

"No, I don't. But suppose there was somebody down there in the mountains who could keep the Bannocks and the Paiutes together and disciplined. Suppose he could make a feint that would draw us away from the post? We've got several hundred thousand rounds of ammunition at the post now, and five hundred new rifles."

"You make me feel that we should turn right around and head back for the post," Dr. Hanlon said. "You don't really believe that, do you?"

"No, I don't. Or I think I don't. And as for Kilrone's theory ... it's too late now. Moreover, there isn't an Indian anywhere who could do it."

"Not that we know of."

Mellett drew on his cigar and looked at the glowing end. "That's right ... not that we know of."

Down the line a few of the fires were already out. Mellett leaned over his fire and pulled back the biggest of the sticks, then scattered dirt over the small blaze. Smoke rose in the air and he tossed another handful of dirt over a glowing ember.

"I'll take a look around," he said. "Better turn in, Cart. I'm going to push it tomorrow. I'm going to try to reach the rendezvous point ahead of time." He bent over and rubbed out his cigar. "Webb just might need some help."

The stars came out, a coyote questioned the night, and Dr. Carter Hanlon stretched out on his back and looked up at the sky. He was tired, but it was a good tiredness, a weariness of the muscles and not of the nerves. A night's rest and a breakfast, and he would be ready again.

But Mellett's doubts worried him. Charlie was not a man to speak as he had tonight unless he was genuinely upset. And Hanlon had been too long on the frontier to be skeptical about the intuitions of old Indian fighters. They knew when trouble was in the wind. He was thinking of that when he fell asleep.

Mellett got to his feet and went over to the horses. He spoke to them softly, and then went on to where the sentry stood. After he had replied to the challenge they stood together for a few minutes.

Keith was a lean, rather haggard young man with a wry sense of humor. He looked like a college professor, but as a matter of fact he had never gotten beyond the fifth grade. He was known in the troop as a particularly vicious rough-and-tumble fighter, and was one of the best rifle shots on the post. This was his fourth year in the cavalry, all of the time on the frontier. He liked Mellett—first, because he was a fighter; and second, because he was never reckless with his troops. The number of fights Mellett's troop engaged in was as great as any other in the regiment, the percentage of casualties appreciably less.

"Think we'll have a fight this time, sir?" Keith asked.

"Yes."

Keith glanced toward the Captain. "Will we meet the Colonel tomorrow, sir?"

"If all goes well."

Mellett moved on, pausing with each of the guards for a few words. As he neared the last man, on the edge of the junipers, he thought he smelled tobacco smoke. The smell was faint, but tangible. Thomas was a new man, and very cocksure.

"Private," he said sternly, "there will be no smoking on guard duty. I believed I smelled tobacco smoke when I came up here. If I was sure, I should see you court-martialed."

Then in a somewhat easier voice he said, "Don't be a fool, man. A lighted match out here can be seen a long way off. If there was an Indian near you'd have lost your scalp."

Mellett moved on, going back through the junipers to camp. Before Mellett had his boots off, Private Thomas had lighted a cigarette. "Damned old fool!" he muttered. "That's Army for you!"

Red Wolf was a young warrior who had yet to take his first scalp. He had been lying under a low clump of sagebrush for more than an hour, and he had watched the glow of a cigarette. Almost ready to make his move,

he had heard somebody approach, and had listened to
the low murmur of voices. There was now no lighted
cigarette to give him the exact location of the man he
intended to kill.

He waited again as he had waited before. After several minutes the glow of the cigarette appeared again.
Lifting his bow, he put an arrow in place, waited an
instant, and let his breath out easily. Then suddenly he
lifted the bow and shot the arrow.

He heard the thud of the arrow, and was moving
before the man fell. His fingers touched the guard's
cheek, then seized his hair; but as the knife cut into the
skin, the body beneath him convulsed suddenly and
hands clawed up at him. He stabbed wildly and in a
panic; once, twice, three times he thrust the knife deep,
and only after the struggles ceased did he again go
about removing the scalp.

Once that was done, he stripped the body, took up
the rifle and belt, and moved quickly and quietly away.
Half a mile away his horse waited, tied in the deepest
part of a thicket. He had been gone for an hour before
the corporal of the guard found the dead man.

"Bury his cigarette butts with him," Dunivant said the
next morning. "If I told him once, I told him twenty
times."

Chapter 5

There was no set pattern for the layout of a frontier army post. Only the earliest ones possessed any kind of a stockade. There was a central parade ground with the various buildings grouped about it to form a rectangle. Outside this, as if looking over the shoulders of the inner buildings, were others, in no sort of formation. Further away, about five hundred yards in this case, was Hog Town, as it was called.

Along one side of the parade ground were the officers' quarters, a row of frame, stone, or adobe houses that faced the enlisted men's barracks across the way. At the north end, Headquarters, a T-shaped building of stone, looked down the length of the parade ground. To the east was the commissary storehouse, also built of stone; to the west the hospital.

At the south of the parade ground was the long, low store of the sutler, or post trader; behind this the stables, corrals, and hay corrals. Behind the barracks were the blacksmith shop, laundry, and a varied assortment of small buildings.

There was always a Hog Town at all the camps on the frontier. There a soldier could find whatever he wanted—women, gambling, and whiskey predominating. Operating the Hog Town here was Iron Dave Sproul, a man whose reputation had started far back along the line. Iron Dave was big, tough, and mean. He had operated such places in a dozen towns before this.

Iron Dave had come off the streets of lower New York, had served a rugged apprenticeship as a prize fighter of sorts, a gang fighter and strong-arm man before coming west to what promised to be richer fields. As a boy in the streets he had had opportunities to study the origins of power, and more than that, the applications of power. He had also learned that more money was to be had. and less risk, by managing the fighter rather than fighting himself.

At first he ran gambling houses and saloons, then owned some of each; but what he was looking for was the right man. What he wanted was a man through whom he could make money; and secondly, a man who would be a means to political power. He believed he had found both.

Iron Dave, so-called because of his iron-hard fists, knew five Indian dialects and was an expert at sign language. He needed no interpreter in talking to Indians. He also knew where and how to dispense favors; and so during the course of his wandering from army post to army post he had given away a blanket here, a rifle there, and occasionally a bottle of whiskey. And he gave them to warriors.

Making no outward show of friendship with the Indians, he still managed to become known among them as a friend. Finally, and discreetly, he began trading in whiskey and rifles, always selling to those he knew personally, always careful to let no other white man know of his activities.

And then he met Medicine Dog.

Medicine Dog was a man consumed by hatred for the white man, and particularly for the horse soldiers. He had been born of a Sioux warrior and a Bannock woman; his parents had come together in the vicinity of Bozeman when the Bannocks, numbering about five lodges, had drifted back to their ancient hunting grounds for a few weeks in the spring.

Noted first for his skill at stealing horses, Medicine Dog had soon won a reputation as a great warrior. He had fought against Crook on the Rosebud, and participated in the Custer massacre, but these were only the latest of the many battles of which he was a veteran. After the Custer fight on the Little Big Horn, when some of the Sioux had fled to Canada, he had drifted westward to his mother's people, the Bannocks. Within a few days he was associated with a group of malcontents eager to promote a fight with the white man.

With three others, Medicine Dog had ridden to a rendezvous with Iron Dave Sproul, to trade for whiskey and guns. And Iron Dave recognized in the strange Indian those qualities of leadership with which a rare few are gifted.

As the three Indians started away after completing their trade, and as Medicine Dog prepared to follow, Iron Dave called him back. Medicine Dog drew up, then slowly walked his horse back, his black eyes glittering.

"You," Iron Dave said, "some day big chief. You need guns, you come to me."

The Dog had merely looked at him, then turned and rode away, but Iron Dave knew he had planted a seed.

A month to the day, Iron Dave looked up from his desk to see Medicine Dog standing looking at some blankets for sale. It was the first time he had been in the trading post that Iron Dave then operated next to his saloon. After a while, the Indian went out and squatted by the edge of the porch.

Iron Dave followed, seating himself on one of the chairs against the wall. He took out a cigar and lit it. Then he asked, "What do you want?"

"Guns . . . for six men."

"All right."

The Dog turned his head. "Suppose I kill white man?"

Iron Dave squatted on the ground, and with a forefinger he traced a brand in the dust. "My horses and my wagons are marked so," he said, and glanced up at the Indian. "The rest are your business."

He gave Medicine Dog the guns, and fifty rounds of ammunition for each. That had been the beginning.

A few weeks later, when word reached Iron Dave Sproul that an old competitor was planning to open a place across the street from his, Iron Dave got word to the Dog, and when the competitor's wagons came north of Pyramid Lake they were attacked suddenly, the stock driven off, the wagons burned. And with the wagons several barrels of whiskey, the gaming tables, poker chips, cards, and other equipment.

His occasional trips into the desert or mountains were easily explained. He was, he admitted, an amateur prospector. He did not profess to know much about ore, but he liked to prospect. Usually he brought back samples, which he discussed over the bar with miners or prospectors or soldiers.

The fact that he usually drove a wagon or a buckboard he accounted for by commenting that, after all, he was a city boy. He would leave the burros to those who liked them. He preferred to travel in comfort. He usually drove into the Santa Rosas, and everybody knew there was ore there.

His occasional gifts or sales to Medicine Dog enabled the Dog to become a big man among the Bannocks. He had rifles to spare, ammunition, and ponies. Moreover, Iron Dave, by a few carefully placed comments to other Bannocks, let them believe that the horse soldiers feared Medicine Dog. Gradually, Medicine Dog's influence grew; from being a comparative outsider, he soon was sitting in council with the chiefs, and the young bucks gathered around him.

At first Iron Dave was wary of his protégé, but as time went on he became more assured in his dealings with the Indian, and even a little contemptuous. After all, had he not practically created the Dog? Had he not built him into a position of influence?

And Medicine Dog had proved a wily tactician. He wasted no men, he wasted no effort. The blows he struck were few but decisive. His "medicine" was good, and the feeling developed among the Indians that he was a chosen one, that with him victory was assured.

His massacre of Webb and his patrol had been a complete success. Medicine Dog had moved on advance information. He knew how many men were with Webb and how they were armed, and he knew their intended route. The ambush had been a total victory. At the first volley from the Indians nine men fell, one of them being Webb, on whom four Indians had been directed to fire.

Another among the first to fall was the only line sergeant in the troop.

Into the plunging, struggling horses and the shouting cavalrymen, the Indians poured a deadly fire at almost point-blank range. Two more dropped. Another's horse bolted into the ranks of the Indians, where the rider was pulled from the saddle and stabbed to death. The entire action required only fifteen minutes, and not an Indian was killed; only three were wounded.

Medicine Dog knew all about Captain Mellett, and knew of his line of march, but he had no intention of meeting him in the field. Leaving behind a small force to harass Mellett, the Dog started for the post with the main body.

The small group he left behind had definite orders. They were not to engage in a battle. They were to draw the soldiers' fire, get them to expend ammunition. They were to steal or drive off their horses if possible, inflict what casualties they could. Medicine Dog wanted M Troop to return to the post a weary, bedraggled lot, needing ammunition, and exasperated at not having come to grips with the enemy.

If all his plans went well, he hoped to be inside the post buildings, waiting for Mellett's men to line up on the parade ground before the order to fall out.

Medicine Dog aimed high. He wanted not only complete destruction of the force at the post, but the post itself. But the destruction of the post would wait until it had been thoroughly looted. With the arms and ammunition from the fort, he would gather a much larger force and move against Fort Halleck, or against Harney if that seemed easier at the moment.

His force now numbered some two hundred warriors. When the news of his victories got out he would have a thousand, perhaps two thousand.

One thing disturbed him, and it disturbed him because it did not fit ... one of his braves, circling around after the fight with Colonel Webb and I Troop, found the tracks of a lone rider. Back-tracking, the Indian discovered that the rider had seen the bodies of the massacred troop. The Indian had lost the trail of the rider when he attempted to follow him.

Who was the lone rider? Where had he gone? Was he enemy or friend? He rode a shod horse, but so did many Indians, now that some rode stolen or captured horses. The rider had walked his horse away from the massacre, and seemed to be in no hurry to get wherever he was going.

No matter ... Medicine Dog headed for the post, unaware that Major Frank Bell Paddock, with sixty men, was headed north, toward him.

And also unaware that the post lay exposed and seemingly helpless, defended by no more than fourteen men.

A cool wind was blowing from the north, and the sky was cloudy. Riding beside Paddock was Hank Laban, fur trapper, buffalo hunter, and scout. He was a thin, angular man with a sour expression but a wry sense of humor. He had phrased his arguments against this march briefly and concisely, and when they were not acted upon he had saddled his fastest horse. There was, he told himself, a time for fighting and a time for running, and he wanted to be ready to run.

"There's been talk," he said suddenly. "I caught me a whisper or two of some new Injun who's cuttin' a wide swath among the Bannocks. Seems like he took some scalps on the Little Big Horn an' he's been tellin' the Bannocks how easy it was to kill white sodgers. I had a look for him but never could get a chance to see how he shaped up, but from what they say he's one mean, smart Injun."

Paddock offered no comment. He was beginning to feel the saddle; that came from too much desk duty. There were always rumors, and he took no stock in them.

"Buffalo Horn is the chief," Pryor commented. "He's said to be over in Oregon."

"Maybe."

Almost another mile had passed before Hank Laban ventured another comment. "Seems this here Injun has him a lot of rifles. All a warrior had to do is say he'll ride along with him and he gets a new rifle with ammunition. I got no idea where he gets them ... Medicine Dog, I mean."

Paddock looked at Laban. "Did you say Medicine Dog? He was supposed to be the one who hit those wagon trains a few months back."

"He's a mean one," Laban repeated.

He rode away suddenly, without further comment, galloping on ahead, then slowing down to sweep back and forth hunting for Indian sign. He found none ... although he did see the tracks of Kilrone's horse, heading south for the fort.

Laban had not met Kilrone, but by the time the column moved out, his arrival was common gossip around the post, and the word was that he had once been an officer in the Army. Laban wondered about Kilrone, absently, without any real concentration of thought. What really disturbed him was the Dog, but he did not seem able to get his worries across to Paddock.

Hank Laban knew enough about Indians to trust his instincts, and his every sense told him that Medicine Dog was a bad one. Paddock had been a fool to leave the post, but you don't tell an army major he's a fool ... not if you want to work for the army; and Laban liked the salary, liked the easy living and the available ammunition.

He liked none of this. Charles Mellett was perfectly capable of taking care of himself with the number of men he had. Just the same, Laban knew he would rather be where he was than back at the post.

Despite the gray day the air was clear, and he could see far off. But his eyes kept straying toward the rear, and he knew what he was looking for. He was expecting to see the smoke of burning buildings.

At the noon halt, Laban squatted by the fire, holding a cup of coffee. "Major," he said, "I ain't one to interfere, but you're on a wild-goose chase. You ain't about to trap that Injun."

"I will be the judge of that," Paddock replied brusquely.

"Major," Laban insisted, "he ain't no common Injun, this here Medicine Dog. You ask me, he's too smart to tackle Charlie Mellett. He'll hit the post, sure as shootin'."

"With seventy-five soldiers waiting for him? That's what he would expect. He certainly can't know that we've marched out from the post."

"He'll know. This Injun gets information right off. You can just bet that by this time he knows."

Information? But how? Doubt assailed Paddock. Almost at once he thought of Mary Tall Singer, Denise's friend. After all, he argued, she was an Indian.

Suppose Laban was right? Suppose Kilrone had been right? If this Indian, this Medicine Dog, should attack the post now there was no chance it could be successfully defended. Sergeant Ryerson was in command until Rybolt returned from Halleck, or one of the detachments returned. Ryerson was a good man . . . but he was ill.

Barney Kilrone was there . . . or had he pulled out? For the first time in hours, Paddock thought of Denise. Suppose Barney took her away with him?

Denise there at the fort. . . . He had not permitted himself to think of what could happen if the post was attacked. He had thought only of the trap he could spring on the hostiles, of the victory he could win, and of the probable results of that victory.

Hank Laban got to his feet. "I'll scout on ahead," he said. "I don't like the feel of things, Major."

"All right . . . go ahead." Paddock got up slowly. His legs felt stiff, and he was sore from the unaccustomed riding.

God, what he wouldn't give for a drink!

Chapter 6

It was mid-morning when Barney Kilrone opened his eyes. For several minutes he lay still, adjusting himself to his surroundings. He had seen Frank Paddock leave with the detachment, and then at the urging of Denise and Betty he had agreed to lie down for a few minutes. He had slept for five hours.

Clasping his hands behind his head, he considered the situation. Paddock might be right, and he might trap Medicine Dog and administer a crushing defeat on the Indians. But that was not the way to figure it. What if the Dog survived, or evaded the fight? Suppose the Dog was the master tactician the Indians were saying he was?

Barney Kilrone had a fast, durable horse. The way west was clear. He could saddle up and ride west and south for Virginia City. He was no longer in the cavalry, and the problem of the post was not his problem. Even if he got into hostile country, the chances were that he could slip through, just as he had in coming here. One man alone, particularly if that man knew how to travel cross-country, had a good chance to get through.

Yet even as he considered the possibility, he knew he would not do it. His duty was clear. He must remain at the post until one of the detachments returned. His rifle might make a difference.

Defending the entire post was out of the question with the few men they had. They must gather all the people into one or two buildings, get enough ammunition, food, and water there for an extended siege.

There was a tap on the door, and he swung his feet to the boards and stood up. "Come in!"

It was Denise. "You're awake, then. Would you like breakfast?"

Betty Considine was still there, and for the first time he really saw her. A slender but well-rounded girl with a lovely face, tanned from sun and wind . . . but not too much.

"How is your shoulder?" she asked.

"Stiff. Thanks for changing the dressing."

It was very still, the only sound the ring of a hammer on metal from the blacksmith shop. The constant under-current of movement, the vague rustle and stir of an army post was lacking. Now the clang of the black-smith's hammer only served to emphasize the unnatural stillness.

"Who is in command?" Kilrone asked.

"Sergeant Ryerson, I suppose," Denise said. "Lieu-tenant Rybolt should be back at any time."

"Tim Ryerson?"

"Do you know him?"

"He was in my outfit in Arizona."

Then they talked casually about many things, remem-bering people and places, talking of army posts other than this, and of Paris during and after the Franco-Prussian War, when Frank Bell Paddock and Barnes Kilrone had been present as observers, with semi-official positions but at their own expense.

The coffee was good, and Kilrone was content to stretch out his legs under the table and to talk quietly, though always as he talked there was the nagging thought in the back of his mind that their time might be running out.

Over the roofs of the barracks he could see the gray sky. The night would be dark, a night without moon, without stars. The wind stirred gently, a wind that would cover the sound of any approach.

He looked up the parade ground toward the Head-quarters building. It was strong, thick-walled, a place where a defense might be made, and the post ware-house was right along side.

For just a little while it was a quiet time in a pleasant

room, and Barney Kilrone, in these last few years, had known few such times. Denise was talking of Zola, and how he had infuriated her father. Yet when his new books came out, he was among the first to buy them, grumbling as he did so.

Kilrone got up suddenly. "I've got to talk to Sergeant Ryerson. Did I understand he was in the hospital?"

Betty Considine got up to join him. "I have to see him, so I'll take you there. The Sergeant has been very ill. He had pneumonia."

They walked together in silence toward the hospital. The farrier working at the blacksmith shop had finished whatever it was he had been doing, and without the sound of the hammer on the anvil the post seemed dead, deserted.

The wind stirred and the leaves of a cottonwood rustled, but there was no other sound except that of their footsteps.

"It's eerie." Betty said, "after so much activity."

"You said the Sergeant had been ill. How is he now?"

"He has been up, sitting in a chair. I don't think he could walk very far yet. He had a very bad attack, and Uncle Carter was afraid we would lose him."

"He's a good man." They walked on a few steps. "Can you shoot?" he asked suddenly.

"Yes." She looked up at him. "Do you think we'll be attacked?"

"Yes, by tonight or tomorrow. We've got one chance, as I see it. We've got to get everybody together at Headquarters. I think we might be able to defend that building, the hospital, and the warehouse. If the men are scattered out, we wouldn't have any chance at all."

"You think Frank was wrong, then?"

He shrugged. "Who can say? I doubt if I would have gone, but another man might have done as Frank did."

They found Ryerson propped up in bed, reading a dime novel. His face broke into a smile when he saw Kilrone. "Captain! Well, I'll be damned!"

"It's been a long time, Tim."

Ryerson gave a sharp glance at Kilrone's shabby cowhand's outfit. "You're out of the army?"

"You should remember. I didn't get along with an Indian agent, and he had political friends."

"I remember. I didn't know you'd resigned, though, because we went out west about that time." He hesitated. "Captain, Iron Dave's here."

Barney Kilrone had started to speak. He broke off short. "Here?"

Suddenly he thought he began to see a pattern, a pattern of action and planning ... but he must be wrong. Except that it was Sproul, and one should never underestimate the man. He was cold, dangerous, and utterly without principle, dedicated to his own interests and to nothing else.

"Has he got a place around here?" he asked.

"Over in Hog Town—the Empire. Be careful, Captain. Once he knows you're out of the army he'll be gunning for you. He only side-stepped you before because he knew he'd have the whole army on his neck. You watch your step."

"Has he been trading with Indians?"

"He has a trading post alongside the Empire, but he makes no point of it. He stays right around the Empire except when he's prospecting."

"*Prospecting?* Iron Dave Sproul?"

"That's right. He's really got the bug. He's out every chance he gets ... and he's come in with some good stuff, I hear."

Sproul . . . Sproul had been the man behind that crooked Indian agent, but so far behind that he was untouchable.

"Do you know him?" Betty asked Kilrone.

"He knows him all right," Ryerson commented grimly. "Sproul threatened to shoot him on sight, and the Captain was going to give him the chance ... but the Old Man wouldn't have it. He confined the Captain to quarters." He looked thoughtfully at Kilrone. "Sproul bragged that you were afraid to come in. He said he wouldn't even use a gun, that he'd break you with his hands."

"I didn't know that." Kilrone felt the old anger rising in him. He had to admit it was not only because of what he knew or suspected about Sproul—that the man had been selling guns and whiskey to the Indians—but something more than that. Iron Dave Sproul was one of those men who had merely to enter a room to raise the hackles on the back of Kilrone's neck.

The man was a brute, physically and mentally, and he carried himself with a hard-shouldered assurance that for Kilrone was like waving a red flag at a bull. Several times soldiers had been found in the alley behind his place who had been brutally beaten, but nothing could ever be proved. One of those soldiers had been a man from Kilrone's own company.

"Tim," Kilrone said, "I haven't any official position here, of course, but Major Paddock is gone and I know you can use every rifle you can get. I think we are going to be attacked.

"I've been thinking about it."

"If you don't mind a suggestion . . ."

"Captain, I'd welcome any suggestion you'd make."

"Pull everybody back to Headquarters. Man that building, the warehouse, and the hospital. You haven't men enough to defend the whole post."

"What about the horses?"

"Forget about them. If there's an attack you couldn't protect them, anyway."

"How much time do you figure we've got?"

"Until tonight or tomorrow, I think. but I'd be moved within the hour. You can't afford to risk it."

Kilrone went outside and stood in the light drizzle that had begun to fall. So Sproul was here, after all this time. Iron Dave Sproul, whose fists had killed at least one man and who prided himself on his ability to fight bar-room style.

There were many such men as Sproul, and Kilrone had met them before this: men who came west, bringing nothing with them but the lust for gold, the desire to get rich and get out; men who would stop at nothing to get what they wanted. But few came as well equipped for what he planned to do as Iron Dave.

Aside from the cunning of the man, and his sheer physical strength and stamina, he was a man of considerable intelligence, and possessed a will for survival earned in the bitter struggles of New York's slums of the 1840's. Barney Kilrone was uncertain as to what Sproul's eventual goal might be, but he was sure that it was more than mere money. The man wanted power ... and perhaps something more than that. There was more behind his conniving than the desire to sell whiskey and rifles to the Indians.

Sproul was careful to keep himself in the clear. It might be that, like many other man, he saw the possibilities in frontier politics? Certainly, Sproul's early background had been a place where politics was part of the power struggle, and he had learned his tricks in a rough but practical school.

Betty had stayed behind to prepare the hospital to receive casualties, but Barney Kilrone wanted to see more of his surroundings. He walked along the line of buildings, spoke to the farrier, who was still in the smithy, and then crossed to the corral where his horse was.

He was turning away from the corral when he saw the Indian girl. Mary Tall Singer was dressed as any American girl of the period would be. She was a pale copperskinned girl with dark, beautiful hair and large eyes. That she was Indian he knew at once.

He spoke to her, and she turned her dark eyes on him, seeming somewhat embarrassed or frightened, though why he could not guess.

"I am Barney Kilrone," he went on. "I rode in yesterday."

"I know. I am Mary Tall Singer." Then she added, "I work for the sutler."

The way in which she spoke and her composure, now that she was past her immediate embarrassment, told him that she not only had education but was accustomed to being treated by whites as an equal.

"You're fortunate. It could be a good job."

"It is. I enjoy my work." She hesitated. "Is there some way I can help?"

"I was looking for a buckboard. Is there one on the post?"

"No. The only one I know of belongs to Mr. Sproul." Yet even as she spoke she seemed to be sorry she had said it. "The only one I know of, that is. He might lend you his."

"I didn't want one right now. I was just curious." He had started away but suddenly he turned back. "Do you know Medicine Dog?" he asked.

There was no visible change in her expression, but he knew at once that she did know him. Her manner was suddenly wary, her eagerness to be away was obvious.

"Medicine Dog," Kilrone said, "is borrowing trouble for himself and his people. I wish he was half as bright as Chief Washakie."

"Do you know Washakie?"

"I know him. I have eaten in his lodge. I have smoked the pipe with him. He is a good man who will do well for his people."

She made no reply, and tipping his hat he went on to the sutler's store.

Hopkins, the sutler, was putting together several sacks of food and ammunition. He glanced up when Kilrone entered. "If you want anything," he said, "find it and bring it up to me." Then realizing that Kilrone was a stranger, he said, "You must be the man who brought the news. Too bad ... there were good men in I Troop. And Webb ... I won't say the man knew much about Indians, but he was a good commander. He kept the post in shape."

Hopkins looked around. "Mary!" he called, then turning back to Kilrone, he said, "I wonder where that girl got to?"

"I saw her down by the corrals."

"Mary? What in God's name would she be doing down there?" he exclaimed.

Kilrone went behind the counter and hunted out a

couple of boxes of shells, considered a moment, and
added two more. The chances were that there would be
plenty of army ammunition but he had no wish to run
short. He added to the ammunition several shirts, hand-
kerchiefs, and odds and ends of clothing.

When he had bundled up the lot he paid for it and
went to the door. There he paused, looking up the
parade ground. Two women were walking toward Headquarters building, each carrying a bundle.

"It looks as if there might be mineral in those hills," he
commented. "Is there much prospecting going on?"

"Here and there."

"When this is over I may have a try at it. I hear that
the fellow who owns the Empire prospects a little."

Hopkins gave him a cynical look. "If you can call
riding around over the country in a buckboard prospecting, he does it. Oh, he comes in with some samples now
and again, but he never looks as if he's done any serious
digging. I never even seen him with his hands dirty."

"Maybe he doesn't stay out long. I knew an old boy
down state who used to go out, find a nice steady place,
and curl up for a sleep. It was the only way he could get
away from his wife."

Hopkins grinned. "Sproul doesn't have a wife. No, he
doesn't stay out long. Overnight, usually. Maybe he just
wants to get away from the Empire. It's a noisy place."

Kilrone took his bundle and started up the street.
Glancing toward the corrals, he saw no sign of Mary
Tall Singer.

He had learned a little. Iron Dave Sproul did not take
his prospecting very seriously, and it was he who drove
a buckboard, accounting for the tracks over in the Santa
Rosas. Suddenly he wanted very much to back-track
that buckboard to see just where it stopped. Without a
doubt Iron Dave was up to his old tricks of peddling
rifles and whiskey to the Indians, but to prove it would
not be easy. How many lives, both Indian and white, had
already been lost due to Sproul's activities?

The rain continued. It fell softly, whispering against
the barrack walls and falling gently upon the ground

where the troops had paraded before they marched off ... I Troop to die, M Troop to what destiny? That was the thing about being a soldier—he never knew when the band played and the girls waved the troop good-bye whether he would ride back or not. He never knew if this good-bye was his last, but there was something about it, something bold and strong that made a man feel his strength, and so he rode and was glad to ride, although he grumbled to be in tune, and let no one know just how he felt.

It was too quiet here, Kilrone was thinking. He could feel trouble coming, for its breath has a way of being felt in the air, and he could feel it now. Whether Iron Dave Sproul was to blame or not, that must wait. First there would come the fight, a good fight, too, if they were to last it out.

How many warriors would come? Two hundred at least, he was sure, and more likely a thousand. And at the post were fourteen or fifteen men and some women, too small a party by far to defend the place, even to defend themselves, despite the fact that there was food enough and ammunition enough.

Suppose he went to Hog Town now? Suppose now, before the fight could begin, he went to see Iron Dave and smashed him down? Or even killed him?

It would change nothing. Whatever influence Sproul had among the Indians would not reach to even one squaw, once the battle was joined. He could not stop them then even if he wanted to, and it was not likely that he wanted to.

What was it the man wanted? There was no one out here who mattered to him unless it was Kilrone himself; and Sproul had not even known Kilrone was in this part of the country, or that Kilrone had been tracking him down, following him from place to place, learning a little here, a bit more there.

Whatever it was he wanted, he needed an Indian war to bring it about.

Chapter 7

Barney Kilrone walked back to Paddock's quarters. Denise had the door open, and a carpetbag was sitting on the step. "May I help?" he asked.

"Would you?" She brought some blankets to the door and handed them to him. "You think Frank was wrong, don't you?"

He shrugged. "I wouldn't have gone, Denise, but I might have been wrong, very wrong. Frank was the one who had the decision to make and he made it. We can only wait and see what happens."

Taking the blankets, Denise's rifle, and the carpetbag, he walked beside her to the Headquarters building.

"This is a long way from Paris," he commented. "Do you miss it?"

"Occasionally. I would be lying if I did not admit it, but I do not miss it nearly so often as one would believe. It is beautiful here ... I love to ride, and I have books to read. Betty is a great help. She's remarkable in so many ways."

She looked to the hills. "And the hills are the best of it all, I think. Frank hates the post. I believe he hates it most because he thinks I do. As a matter of fact, I love those mountains; they're so restful, so ... enduring, and timeless."

Stella Rybolt was waiting for them inside the door. "Well, you made it!" she said cheerfully to Denise. "I was just coming down to lend a hand."

"Stella Rybolt, this is Barnes Kilrone. It used to be Captain Barnes Kilrone."

"How do you do, Captain? Oh, I remember you! We never met, but there were stories, Captain, there were stories! And such stories!"

51

"Better forget the 'captain'," Kilrone suggested. "That was several years ago. I'm a civilian now."

"I wish Gus was here. You were a favorite of his. He liked the way you took after that Indian agent back down the line. Said we needed more officers like you."

"And I'm no longer in the army because of it," he commented dryly. "I'll admit nobody forced me to resign, but there were things I wanted to do that I could not do while in uniform. So I resigned and did them."

"I know." Stella Rybolt gestured toward the pot-bellied stove. "Look, I've made some coffee. Let's sit down and talk a little. It's no use sitting around with long faces."

Kilrone shifted his feet. "Later. I have a few things to do."

As he stepped outside, one of the farriers walked up to him. "Kilrone? I'm McCracken. Sergeant Ryerson said you'd be acting in command."

"McCracken, I'm going to put you and your partner, Dawson, in the warehouse. Webster will be with you. I don't need to tell you that those Indians mustn't get the warehouse."

"They won't, sir."

"You'll be getting help from us. We can cover you front and back from Headquarters. We'll have to be helping the boys in the hospital, too. And you can help us. But don't forget to watch your blind side."

"Are you planning to release those boys from the guardhouse? They're good fighters, if you can handle 'em. That Lahey, now—he's the best rifle shot in the regiment—or one of the best. And he's a fighter ... believe me, he is."

"How about the other two?"

"Troublemakers, both of them. Teale is a cowhand from Texas. The boys figure he joined up so he'd have a place to stay during the winter."

"A snowbird?"

McCracken grinned. "You know the lingo, sir. Yeah, that's what he is. He's a rider, though, and a good man when he's sober—which is most of the time. When he gets a couple under his belt he heads for Hog Town and a poker game."

"And loses every cent he makes?"

"You said it." McCracken glanced at him. "Do you gamble?"

"When Sproul runs the house it's no gamble, believe me. He never ran an honest game in his life."

McCracken shrugged. "That's a good way to get killed, saying something like that where it can be heard."

"He wants me, anyway," Kilrone replied shortly, "and maybe he'll get his chance."

"The other one over there," McCracken said, "is a Swiss, he says. He might be something else . . . a German or a Pole. There's no telling about some of these people. This one is big and he's mean, but he'll fight. He has made sergeant three times, I hear, and lost his stripes each time. He's only been with us a few weeks. His name is Mendel. At least, that's his name for this enlistment."

The rain continued, but remained a fine, mistlike rain. One by one as the men came up the parade ground he assigned them to their places. The three from the guardhouse he broke up, putting Lahey in the hospital, Teale in Headquarters, and adding Mendel to the warehouse.

Ryerson would remain in command at the hospital, McCracken would handle the warehouse. Reinhardt, a teamster, and Olson, a cook, would also be at the hospital.

With himself at the Headquarters building he would have Kells, Draper, and Ryan, teamsters. Ryan was a brother of one of the men lost with I Troop. He would also have Rudio the baker, Teale from the guardhouse, and Hopkins the sutler. And with them in Headquarters they would have ten women and six children.

"What about Hog Town?" Teale asked.

"They'll get along," Hopkins said. "Dave Sproul has at least twenty men over there. Anyway, it's the post they'll be wanting, and we'll be having plenty of trouble here before this is over."

As the day went on they worked steadily, bringing

food from the warehouse to the hospital and to Headquarters; and a barrel was brought into each place and
filled with water. Sacks from the sutler's store and the
warehouse were brought in to fight fire; and materials
for binding wounds and taking emergency care of in-
juries were brought from the hospital.

All the available weapons on sale at the sutler's were
brought to Headquarters and loaded. With spare rifles
from the warehouse, each man had two rifles.

"How many of you women can load?" Kilrone asked.
"Miss Considine and Mrs. Paddock excepted. I want
them free to handle the wounded, if any."

"I can load," Stella Rybolt offered. "I've had a spell or
two of loading before this."

Alice Dunivant and Sophie Dawson, wives of enlisted
men, could load too. Pat Dunivant, who was twelve, also
volunteered.

As the shadows gathered, Kilrone walked restlessly
about, studying the buildings along the parade ground,
and the hills that loomed just beyond. Without doubt
there was an Indian, and possibly several, already waiting up in the Santa Rosas, an Indian who was watching
whatever they did. As he moved about he tried to think
of anything he might have overlooked. If the attack
lasted long, a barrel of water would not be enough—but
there were no more barrels.

"There's barrels in Hog Town," Teale commented,
grinning tauntingly at Kilrone. "All you got to do is go
get them."

"And I might do just that."

Teale looked at him skeptically. "From Iron Dave?
He'd make you pay five times the price."

"Maybe we can find some others," Kilrone said. "Otherwise, we might have to go get them."

"You," Teale said, "not me."

At Hog Town, Iron Dave Sproul sat at his roll-top desk
and chewed on a long black cigar while he listened to
Poole's report.

"They've pulled out of the barracks," Poole said.

"Hopkins even left his store. They're holed up in Headquarters, the hospital, and the warehouse."

"You say Paddock rode out with sixty men? It doesn't sound reasonable that he would leave the town and the post undefended."

"It ain't likely Medicine Dog would make a try at this place," Poole said. "And Paddock may trap him if he tackles Mellett."

"Who's in command at the post? Rybolt?"

"He ain't due back until tomorrow or the next day." Poole lifted his wary eyes to Sproul's. "He went after the payroll. You'd figure," he added, "he'd not risk it with Indians on the warpath. That there payroll could disappear an' nobody be the wiser."

Sproul rolled his cigar in his jaws, considering that. Of course Poole was right. If the entire payroll guard was wiped out nobody would know how it happened, but the Indians would be blamed. There was risk, but all atrocities were blamed on the Indians anyway. In any event, he had no idea of letting Poole know how he was thinking, for the fewer who knew the better, and he wanted no one around to point a finger in the years to come.

All his trade with the Indians he had handled himself, and so far as he knew not even one of the men who worked for him at Hog Town had any idea of it. The danger had always been that of being caught in the act, but he had moved with care, kept himself informed on troop movements, and had carefully avoided anything that would arouse suspicion. His "prospecting" had been a neat cover.

"Sergeant Ryerson's actually in command," Poole went on, "but there's some newcomer givin' orders around. Some feller I never seen before."

"What's his rank?"

"That's the funny part, Mr. Sproul. This man ain't even in uniform. He's some civilian friend of Paddock's, from what they say."

Sproul was disturbed. A civilian giving orders on an army post? It didn't sound reasonable. In fact, he'd never heard of such a thing ... more than likely it was a mistake. But the unknown or ill-defined always disturbed him. Sproul was a planner, a conniver, and he based his actions on information, and that information he wanted exact and complete. This unknown civilian was a new consideration, and it irritated him that he knew nothing about him.

"What's he look like?"

Poole shrugged. "I seen him around. He looks like some down-at-the-heel cowhand ridin' the grub line. Big, rangy man, wide shoulders, narrow hips ... mighty shabby. He rides a good horse though."

The description told Sproul nothing. It might have been that of any number of men he knew—of a dozen who came to Hog Town on Saturday night.

A friend of Major Paddock? He mulled that over, remembering all he knew of Paddock. He seemed an unlikely person to have a friend, welcome in his home as this one was, who was simply a cowhand, a drifting cowhand at that. And Denise Paddock was French, so that left that out.

After Poole was gone he considered what he had learned, dismissing the stranger for the time being. It was of no real importance anyway, he decided, for they could not hope to defend the post with so few men.

The warehouse was the important building, for if the Bannocks could get the arms that were stored there, they would constitute a threat to the whole frontier. The man who averted that threat would find himself in an enviable position, and one hard to defeat in any election. And it was this toward which Iron Dave Sproul had been working for more than ten years.

Many things could be said about him, but nothing could be proved, for Sproul was not the owner of record of any of the gambling houses or honky-tonks with which he had been associated. He made a practice of coming around, of being seen, and of talking to people here and there. It was assumed he was the owner, and so he was; but in each case he had a straw man between himself and the records.

In the future he would blandly deny any connection with such places. Yes, he had been around them, but they were the customary meeting places on the frontier, and much business was done in saloons and gambling houses. Men met there to buy or sell cattle, to complete mining deals, to arrange for freighting contracts.

Medicine Dog was the key to the outbreak, and it was Sproul who had built him into prominence. When the news was released that Webb had been killed and his troop massacred, then that Medicine Dog had attacked and burned the post, taking over five hundred stands of arms—it was an exaggeration but it sounded well—the frontier would be in a panic.

At that moment, Dave Sproul would step in, meet with the Indians, end the outbreak, and become the man of the hour. From there he might become governor or go to the Senate ... and Dave Sproul knew how politics could be used by a man with no scruples, no moral principles, and only a driving greed and ambition.

Chapter 8

The hours preceding an attack are slow hours. The minutes pace themselves slowly, and those who wait find a savor in life, for they begin to taste, to feel, to hear as at no other time. They realize these hours may be their last, and their senses are sharpened and more alert, and things formerly ignored are now appreciated or at least realized, as never before.

Night came gently to the post. The rain continued quietly. There was no thunder, no lightning, no heightening of drama in so far as nature was concerned.

In the three buildings at the end of the parade ground the people bedded down like refugees, making themselves comfortable, half in fear and half in a sort of thrill at the strangeness of it. To the few youngsters, the atmosphere was almost that of a picnic. It was camping out ... some of them had not even seen the inside of Headquarters before.

Guards were posted outside, none of them further than sixty feet from the buildings. Of one thing they were sure. The Indians would not come with a rush, exposing themselves as targets. They would come quietly, moving like shadows in the earliest hours before the dawn, or perhaps even at night. They would be close and all around them before anyone realized it. The men on guard post knew they would have little time in which to get back inside; the last guard of the night would be mounted from within the buildings.

Kilrone had too few men for any offensive action. He could afford no losses. His would be a holding action, an attempt to delay until the patrols could return. The tactical advantages of defense were denied him, for he had no covering forces to use in delaying the enemy, to

58

disorganize their advance, or decieve them as to the true location of the defense.

His greatest advantage lay in his excellent field of fire to the north and south, and in the covering fire the three buildings could offer for each other. The greatest disadvantage lay in the limited field of fire to east and west.

The women, rising as always to an emergency, when more often than not they function at their best, bustled about and were busy.

He was not worried about the women; he knew that in those around him he was especially fortunate. These were soldiers' wives or relatives, bred to a realization of frontier life and the possibility of frontier warfare. Not one of them was likely to falter.

Stella Rybolt, as the more experienced, was in her element. Denise was quietly competent, quietly in command, but without any effort at assertion. She, who alone among the women had not been born or brought up on the frontier, came of a soldier family; moreover, being of the nobility and the wife of a commanding officer here, hers was a necessity for courage. One of the easiest ways to be brave is to have bravery expected of you.

With Denise there could be no question of her role. The matter of her role or her reaction to the situation would never even arise in her mind, for the position to which she had been bred was not only that of leader, but of protector.

Barney Kilrone walked out on the parade ground, visiting each barracks. It had been the rule to have a barrel of water at each corner of each barracks building, but those barrels were now gone. Inquiry revealed that they had been piled into a wagon and taken to the creek for refilling, and had not been returned. That had been two days ago.

Paddock had been drinking, Ryerson ill, and nobody had been quite up to par. Colonel Webb and Mellett gone ... and somebody had been careless. But it might have been part of a preconceived plan, arranged by someone who was aiming at destruction of the army post. Well, if those barrels had been left at the creek they should be there still.

He went on toward the corrals and stopped. Just ahead of him he heard a faint rustle of movement, glimpsed a momentary shadow. Somebody was pitching hay to the horses. Kilrone walked around the corral and it was Teale.

He stopped when he saw Kilrone, poised with the pitchfork in his hand. "You, is it? Figured I'd feed the horses before I went on guard. They may not get fed for a while."

"Good thinking." Kilrone paused. "Teale," he said after a moment, "we should have those barrels. If this lasts any while at all, one barrel of water for each building won't be enough. Especially at Headquarters, where the women and children will be."

Teale was leaning on his fork now. Because of the darkness, Kilrone could not tell what his reaction was.

"The barrels were left in a wagon down at the creek," Kilrone said. "Would you know where that would be?"

"Uh-huh. There's a pool near the Hog Town crossing. We usually watered up there. When the Major ordered K Troop out, they were told just to leave the wagon, that somebody would go pick it up, but nobody did."

"Catch me up a couple of those mules, will you, Teale? I'm going after that wagon."

"Suppose the wagon ain't there?"

"Then I'll go where it is."

"Alone?"

"Why not? In any event, we can't spare any men to go along. They'll be needed on the post."

Teale stood his fork against the corral. "Maybe they can spare one man. I'd like to sort of trail along an' see what happens."

He paused. "You got any idea what you're gettin' into? I know why that wagon wasn't sent after. Some of Sproul's men hooked onto it and pulled it into Hog Town. Ryerson was too sick to go himself and didn't like to send anybody after it without orders. Now, I've got a feelin' Iron Dave Sproul won't let you have that wagon, and if you make any kind of a fuss, Iron Dave will chop you up without working up a sweat."

Teale stepped into the corral, caught a couple of the big Missouri mules, and led them out. Kilrone shut and fastened the gate while Teale took the mules to the harness rack.

After the animals were harnessed, the two men mounted and rode away toward the creek, Teale leading the way. Kilrone sat silently on the big mule.

Their time was short. Barrels or not, they must get back before daylight. His thoughts strayed to Betty Considine. There was something about her that stuck in a man's mind, some quality beyond her beauty or her charm. It was that quiet competence that made a man realize she was a woman to walk beside a man and not behind him. She had a certain glamor, but she had staying quality also, and it was a quality to look for in horses, in men, or in women.

Trees hung over the creek, shadowing the gently rustling waters. The rain hissed softly as it fell. Otherwise, the night was still. There was no wagon, and the light they struck revealed two deep cuts in the far bank where it had gone up.

Teale blew out the match. "Hog Town," he said. "What'll we do?"

"Why, we'll go to Hog Town, I guess," Kilrone said.

They rode on, and a few steps further along he asked, "What are they like in Hog Town? Gang-fighters?"

"If need be. But no gang piles in when Iron Dave fights. He doesn't need any help."

"Then if I tangle with Dave, you keep the others off, d'you hear?"

"Hell, Sproul wouldn't let them butt in. He likes doing it himself. He'll kill you, *amigo*."

"Teale, one thing you should know. This will be real trouble. I know Dave Sproul and he knows me. He hates my guts. He'll kill me if he can."

"You know him? An' you'll still go over there?" Teale rode along in silence for a few moments. "Hell," he said presently, "I could win all the pay in camp, bettin' on you. They'd offer ten to one."

"Don't get me wrong, Teale. I'm not looking for a fight. We'll have all the fight we can handle if Medicine Dog and his braves come down on us, as I believe they will. There's plenty of time for Dave Sproul."

The one street in Hog Town, no more than a stretch of muddy road, was dark and still. Lights shone from the Empire, and they could hear the sound of a tinny music box as they drew nearer. A few yards from the end of the street Kilrone drew up. "You know this place, Teale. Where would he be likely to have that wagon, if he has it?"

"Now, that's a problem, Cap. It surely is. He'd be likely to have it near the corrals or at the barn, if he was honest about it, but I'd guess he'll have it closer by. Maybe behind the Empire itself."

Teale pointed. "There's a smaller stable there, where he keeps his own horses, and back of that there's cottonwoods and some brush. I'd guess the wagon would be there."

"Well, let's have a look."

Across the street from the Empire was a line of cribs. As the two rode toward the back of the Empire, a man came from one of the cribs and started across toward the saloon.

When he glimpsed the two riders, he stopped dead-still, staring after them. Had he caught a brief glint of brass buttons? Scarcely, in this rain. Anybody out and about tonight would be wearing a slicker. Then why had he felt that one of those men was a soldier?

When Poole went into the Empire he saw no sign of Iron Dave, so he walked to the bar for a drink.

"The army been in tonight?" he asked.

The bartender shook his head. "Ain't likely. They're all gone but a dozen or so, and those who are there will be kept on guard."

"Why, you'd be right about that," Poole agreed. "Give me a shot of that Injun whiskey."

"Injun whiskey? We got the real stuff here. After all, you're one of Dave's boys, so why not?"

"I asked for the Injun. I know what it's made out of, but there's somethin' about it. After all, I've drunk it for years, and nothin' else seems to promise. Maybe it's the chawin' tobacco they shave up in it . . . or that dash o' strychnine."

He accepted the Indian whiskey, tossed off a glass, and refilled it. "Reason I asked about the sodgers, I thought I saw one out there just as I came in."

"You're seein' things."

Iron Dave came in then and walked down the bar. The big saloon was almost empty. The rain and rumors of Indian trouble had kept local people and ranchers away, and the soldiers were all gone.

Sproul was a powerfully built man with thick shoulders, and huge arms and fists. He was dressed like a city man, but was in his shirt sleeves. A massive chain of gold nuggets was draped across the front of his vest. The only incongruous note was the pistol in its holster.

"How are you, Poole?"

"He's seein' things," the bartender said, "an' before he started drinkin'. He claims he saw a soldier just now."

"A soldier? Where?"

"Headed back yonder." Poole indicated the back of the saloon. "There were two men, and I think one of them was a soldier. Too far off to see their faces."

Sproul turned sharply. "Dick! Pete! You and Shack get out there and have a look at the wagon! Quick now!"

He turned on Poole. "Go with 'em! If you see anybody, shoot!"

Poole remained where he was. "I hired on as a scout," he said, "and a guide if need be. But I ain't shootin' at no soldier. Not in uniform, I ain't."

Sproul gave him a hard look. "I'll remember that, Poole."

"Been my experience," Poole said dryly, "that a man who starts trouble with the army usually winds up with the short end of the stick."

Teale led the way almost directly to the wagon with its load of barrels. Quickly they swung the mules into place, lifted the tongue, and hitched up as fast as they could. Kilrone was snapping the trace chains when they heard a door slam.

"Here they come, Teale. Get up on the seat and start the wagon."

"What about you?"

"I'll meet you in front. You swing down along the creek and come around in the street headed back toward the fort. I'll be out front in a jiffy. If anybody tries stopping you . . . shoot."

The team started, and from the edge of the brush there came a shout. The man called Pete came through the brush, lifting a pistol. He did not even see Kilrone until it was too late.

Kilrone's pistol barrel smashed down on Pete's wrist just as he was lifting the gun. He cried out and dropped the gun. Kilrone turned sharply, a pistol flowered with flame not fifteen yards away, and he fired instantly, shifted his position, and fired at a splash of water. Stepping over two feet he waited, listening, while ejecting the spent shells and reloading the empty chambers.

He heard no sound, waited a moment longer, and then rounded a tree and walked back through the brush. Behind him, Pete was moaning and cursing, undoubtedly with a broken wrist. If there had been anyone else there, whoever it was had decided to remain still, not liking the sound of what he had heard.

Kilrone holstered his gun, crossed the back lot, passed the barn, and went up the walk to the back door of the saloon. Opening it, he stepped into a hall perhaps fifteen feet long, and walked along this to another door. When he opened this and went through, he was in the saloon.

The room was empty except for the bartender, a sleepy-eyed man standing at the end of the bar with a bottle, and Iron Dave himself.

"Hello, Dave," Kilrone said mildly. "Still up to your old tricks, I see."

"Kilrone, is it? I might have known it was you. Well, I'm glad you're here. Now we can settle something."

Kilrone shook his head. He stood with his feet a little apart, ready to move quickly. He was listening for the sound of the wagon, and knew there was little time. "I'd like to stay on, Dave, and give you the whipping you've had coming. There really isn't so much iron in you, Dave, and what there was has been turning soft, or you wouldn't be fool enough to think you can get away with this."

"With what?"

"Your plotting with Medicine Dog."

Kilrone said this because he knew Dave Sproul. He knew how the man thought, or believed he did, and it would be like him to use the Dog—if he could. "It's obvious enough, you know. But what you don't seem to grasp is that the Dog may turn on you. He isn't to be trusted, maybe even less than you are."

"I'm going to kill you," Iron Dave said, matter-of-factly, "and this time you don't have the Army to hide behind."

Kilrone heard the sound of the wagon and went toward the door. "As I said, I haven't time now. Later, if the Indians don't come or if they leave anything behind, I'll come around and give you a thrashing. And don't try reaching for that gun. I'm much faster than you."

Kilrone had the feeling that both the bartender and the other man were enjoying the scene. Neither offered to move. He backed to the door, glanced quickly around, then stepped outside, and as the wagon went sweeping by, he jumped for the tailgate and swung himself up.

The door of the Empire was flung open and Kilrone put a bullet into the door jamb, a move to restrain anyone who might think of taking a shot after them.

The rain had ceased, and the night was still. At the creek they stopped, filled the barrels, and drove on back to the fort. They unloaded the water barrels and with help from inside, rolled them into place.

Kilrone rode to the end of the parade ground with

Teale and together they stripped the harness and returned it to the racks.

"Not that it's likely to matter," Teale commented. "The Indians will steal most of it if they come."

They stood together, listening into the night. The rain had begun again, fine, whispering, not unpleasant. At the far end of the parade ground lights glowed from the windows.

"What happened back there?"

"Nothing ... Only he knows I'm here now, and he'll be waiting for me when this is over." They started to walk along together. "It's a long story, Teale. I found an Indian agent shorting the Indians on rations ... he had a deal with Sproul. And Sproul had a corner of land near the post area for his layout—just as he has here.

"He had political power, and I didn't, but I did have a friend in Congress. I got him to amend the bill by which they located the post so that they would take in fifty acres more.

"Nobody protested . . . it seemed an unimportant thing at the time, but that additional fifty acres had Sproul's place on it, and the change in the bill put that land under government supervision.

"I knew he was selling whiskey to the Indians, but I couldn't prove it. Two of my men—and that was what really started me going—had been robbed and murdered over there. Yet there was no way to get at him. He always had his trail well covered, and he had political connections. The Colonel who was in command at the fort wanted a promotion and would do nothing about it. But there came a time—he was all right, that Colonel—when he got leave to go East and I was left in command."

Teale glanced at him with sudden interest. "And you did it? You got rid of him?"

"The place was a corner, you see? On one side, the river, on the other the government land occupied by the post. He was hedged in. He had gone to Cheyenne ... he went there regularly ... so I simply moved in, jacked up his smaller buildings—they were all frame, you know ...

used timbers and artillery caissons—and moved the whole lot five miles south and left them on the bank of the river. It was fifteen miles around the head of a deep canyon and in the middle of desolation."

Teale chuckled. "I'd like to have seen his face!"

"He got back at night and found his place gone. There had been five buildings, only one of them of any size. The others were mere shacks. But he couldn't find his town. It took him three days, because I'd given orders that no civilians could cross the post without a written permission from the Colonel, and the Colonel was in New York by that time."

They were standing outside Headquarters now. "What happened?" Teale asked.

"By the time the Colonel returned I had some evidence. Not a thing against Sproul, you understand—his tracks were well covered, but I found enough on the Indian agent to urge his dismissal. Well, he was dismissed, all right, but I was transferred to another post ... and then I resigned."

"You kind of stretched yourself," Teale commented. "It took nerve to buck the army and Sproul at the same time."

"Teale, you watch this man's army and you'll notice something. They'd rather have action than inaction, any time. It may not always be that way, but that's the way it is now. If you're in doubt, plunge in. Believe me, if I'd stayed in I might have been shifted around a while until the political boys forgot me, and then I'd have been in the running again . . . maybe. Only I was always a rebel, and I wanted Sproul's scalp. In the army I'd have had to leave him alone."

"Now that he knows you're here," Teale said, "you watch your step." He was about to go inside, then he paused. "Cap, if there's any way I can help ... watch your back or anything ... you count me in. Believe me, you can count on any of the boys in this fight. You'll see."

"Thanks ... thanks, Teale."

Kilrone stood alone in the darkness and the rain. He

was going to need them ... he was going to need them all, not against Sproul, but against Medicine Dog. That was why he had talked as much as he had. They needed to know something about him, they needed to know who they were taking orders from.

The enemy would be out there by now ... Medicine Dog, his Bannocks, and his renegades. They would be out there, waiting.

Chapter 9

Denise Paddock stepped from the dark doorway and stood beside him. "Barnes ... will he be all right?"

"Of course."

"But he hasn't ridden a patrol in months, and he's been drinking."

"He's a good soldier, Denise, and a brave man. This may be just what he needs."

Barney Kilrone spoke the words and he made them sound sincere. Actually, he felt that Frank Bell Paddock had made a ghastly mistake. His long ride would come to nothing. He would effect his junction with Mellett and they would then return to the post ... to what?

Denise stood silent, and all the past stood between them. How far, he thought, from the night they danced together for the first time at Combourg!

"I wish it were spring," she said suddenly. "I dread the thought of winter."

"I don't blame you. This is one of the coldest places in the country." He was listening as he spoke, but the soft drizzle of rain deadened any sound. Yet he had the feeling ... he knew they were out there.

How long before Mellett and Paddock could return, he was thinking. Three days? Four?

"Remember Brittany in the spring?" Denise said. "I liked it better than in Paris, I think."

"It was a time of innocence," he said. "That spring, I mean. By the time autumn came around, everything had changed."

"Have you ever thought of what might have happened?" She looked at him curiously.

"Of course ... but nobody can say when the turning point comes. Suppose instead of coming to Combourg that night I had decided—which I almost did—to go on? There's no use thinking about it. If one thing changes, everything is changed. At Combourg I met you . . . we had stopped there only by chance. That began it, you might say. And then we met again ... It was three weeks before I returned to Paris."

"And after that when we met again I was married to Frank Bell Paddock."

"And happily so."

The trouble was, Frank Paddock had known about them, but what he did not seem to realize was that for Denise, Frank Paddock was the only man with whom she could have been happy. Certainly, Kilrone admitted, she could not have been happy with him. He knew that and Denise knew it, and neither had regrets. The trouble was, Frank had never believed it.

"He's out there now because of us," Kilrone said bitterly.

"No, he's not." Denise spoke firmly. "I love Frank, but what he has become is his own fault. And whatever he does in the future will be up to him."

The sensible view, but was it the true one? "All that was long ago and far away . . . another world than this."

"What are you going to do, Barnes?"

He shrugged. "If I get out of this? I don't know. Settle somewhere in the West, I expect. This country grows on me, and I doubt if I'd be content anywhere else."

Denise went back inside then, and once more he was alone in the darkness. He should be getting some rest while it was possible, but he was in no mood for it. A deep restlessness was upon him. He knew their chances were slight. Such defenses had been made before this, but in other instances the position had been better than the one they now held. If he had a larger force . . .

He squatted on his heels against the wall where there was shelter from the slight rain. With each succeeding minute the time of attack was drawing nearer, and any possible help was miles away. Worst of all, somewhere en route from Fort Halleck was Lieutenant Rybolt with the payroll and its handful of guards.

That payroll must come to quite a lot of money. It was unlikely that such a move would have gone unnoticed by either the Indians or the men at Hog Town; and such a sum, at such a time, would be tempting. But there was nothing to be done about it. With Ryerson in poor health, Kilrone must stay on. He would have remained in any case because his rifle was needed here.

The door of the warehouse opened noiselessly, and closed. A dark figure moved toward him. It was McCracken.

"Kilrone?"

McCracken moved closer. "I figured that was you. How much time do you reckon we've got?"

"An hour ... maybe two." Kilrone pondered the situation a moment. "Better get Webster busy on something for you boys to eat—coffee, and a quick, light breakfast, with at least two men always on watch; but whatever you have to eat, take it to your posts with you."

"I was going to ask about that." McCracken squatted beside him. Finally, he said, "You reckon we got a chance?"

"We've got a good chance," Kilrone replied with an assurance he did not feel. "Look what those boys did at Adobe Walls a few years back—twenty-eight buffalo hunters stood off upwards of seven hundred Indians. Some say as many as fifteen hundred."

McCracken stood up. "Well, I'd hate to have it happen like this. I've got a family back in the States, but I've taken bigger risks for less ... considering those folks in there." He gestured toward the Headquarters building behind them.

"Take your time, make every shot count, that's all anybody can do."

When McCracken had left, Kilrone got up and walked to the hospital, eased in, and talked to Ryerson. He saw that several cases of ammunition and food had been brought over from the warehouse. Everything looked ready. Only then did he return to the silent Headquarters and stretch out on the floor, lying on his bedroll. Almost instantly he was sleeping.

Major Frank Bell Paddock, camped near Twin Buttes, at the head of Toppin Creek, could look north toward his destination, still a hard day's ride from where they were. They could not wait as long as a night here. Four hours of rest, he decided, with a chance for the horses to graze; then up, a light breakfast, and in the saddle once more.

Hank Laban squatted on his heels near the fire, a little apart from the others. He held his cup in both hands, and sipped the hot black coffee with slow pleasure. He was a coffee-drinking man, and he relished these minutes by the fire, which were too few. He was a man without illusion, looking on life with ironic appreciation of its realities, and watching with a jaundiced and half-amused eye those who viewed life through the mist of their own desires, fears, or ambitions.

Nor had he any illusions about Indians. He knew them and, generally speaking, liked them. He had lived their life and found much of it good; but he knew that the red man, like his white brother, could be led down the garden path by a good talker. And somebody had been stirring the Indians into trouble. Buffalo Horn was one thing—he was torn between leading his people in a rightful fight for Camas Prairie, where they had dug the camas roots from times unknown, and his own desire to outdo Chief Joseph. But Buffalo Horn was already a half-tame Indian. Medicine Dog was another matter: he was not tame.

The Dog was a broncho Indian. Like Geronimo, he was not a chief, merely a warrior who attracted to himself the unsettled youngsters, eager to make themselves big Indians, the malcontents, and the hardheads who refused to know when they were whipped. The Dog was tough, mean, and cunning as a wolf, dangerous as a prairie rattler.

Nothing was ever simple any more. Hank Laban would have liked to ride with Mellett. Mellett was a soldier, pure but far from simple. He was smart and direct, and when he hit he hit hard, and no nonsense. Paddock was a good enough man when sober, and he was sober now, but Paddock wasn't simply riding after Indians, he was riding after a reputation. Laban was an old coon from the high-up creeks, and he knew the signs.

Young Pryor was riding for the same reason, only where Paddock was desperate and at the end of his tether, Pryor was bursting at the seams to fight somebody, anybody. He wanted glory—or what he thought would be glory—and he wanted promotion. He wouldn't even mind a scar if he got it in a romantic-seeming place. Pryor was impatient with all of them—with Mellett, with Paddock, with Webb. Ride right out and ride the Indians into the ground—that was his idea. What he wanted was a cavalry charge, and he bitterly regretted that the saber was no longer used on the western prairie.

Hank Laban continued to sip his coffee, and he speculated on his horse. That was a fast-running horse he had. Come to the worst, he might make it out ... and if it came to the worst, he was going to try. He did not like to ride with ambition. He wanted to ride with soldiers, with fighting men doing a fighting job, solid, steady men who fought to win, but fought with common sense, not bravado and dash. That sort of thing could get a man killed.

In a lifetime on the frontier Hank Laban had managed to keep his scalp. He had held onto his hair by fighting when he could, running when he could no longer fight, or lying quiet when outnumbered. He was a disciple of the philosophy that nothing has to be done all at once.

The fact that they were riding away from where he believed most of the Indians to be made him no happier. He had never gotten used to seeing the ravished and scalped bodies of men, and especially those of women and children. In his own mind he was gospel sure that was what they would find on returning to the post. He was not reconciled to the idea of riding where they were riding; he knew they'd find Indians enough themselves, and they'd find them when they least wanted them.

The canyon of the Owyhee was rough and rugged. This whole country was rough. Earthquakes and volcanoes in prehistoric times had had their way with the land, and they had upset it here, ruptured it there. It was ambush country, no mile of it safe. Hank Laban had lost nothing on the North Fork, and he wanted to lose nothing there, least of all, his scalp.

The risks he had accepted when he took the job. He had ridden with good men, and he had ridden with the glory-hunters and the hardheads. A man had to take it as it came.

Paddock walked back to the fire and sat down on a rock, stiff and saddle-sore. He looked over at Laban. "You think we're on a wild-goose chase?" he asked.

"Yep."

"We won't find any Indians?"

"Oh, you'll find Indians, all right. You'll find a passel of them when you want 'em least. Only you won't find the Dog. Right about now he's burning your post."

"Nonsense!" Pryor said sharply. "No Indian would dare attack an army post!"

Hank Laban did not bother to reply. He almost never bothered to reply to Lieutenant Eden Pryor, and the Lieutenant was growing irritated. He resented Laban's attitude and his own inability to impress the scout. Pryor disliked Laban's careless, almost slovenly appearance as much as he disliked the respect that all the older soldiers gave to his opinions.

Paddock smoked in silence for a few minutes and then suggested, "Laban, why don't you sketch out the route for me? I've never been over this trail before."

Laban hunched forward and took up a twig from the edge of the fire. He poked in the ground. "Here we are. We'll cross the upper canyon of the Little Owyhee right about here," and he drew the line in the sand. "Then we'll strike out for Pole Creek. Over yonder there's a travois trail and we'll follow it right up into the corner here where the Owyhee and the Little Owyhee join up."

He made a cross in the sand "Right there, Major, we may run into plenty of grief. There's an Injun trail down the cliffs—the boys will have to hoof it and lead their hosses. Now, I say there's a trail. It's just a rock slide, and if the shelf along there should topple over some of that trail would be gone. I mean, if the trail's still there we'll take it. Ever' time I go that way I expect to find it gone.

"That's rough country with a lot of weathered rock," he went on, "and if a few feet of it should go we'd be up the creek. Well, we go down that slide, an' we'll have a time. What we'd best do is put a few men on the rim and then send a few more down below to cover us. If those Injuns catch us on that slide they'll cut us in half."

"Then why do we go that way?" Pryor interrupted.

"After we cross the plateau between the rivers, we'll still have the Middle Fork to cross. From there on it's ten, twelve miles to where Mellett will be."

"I asked you why we didn't go around." Pryor's tone was coldly furious.

Paddock looked up sharply. "Lieutenant Pryor, Mr. Laban is explaining a route to me. I would be pleased if you would not interrupt."

Pryor started to reply, then stood up and turned away abruptly. Corporal Steve Blaine, who had no particular liking for Pryor, nonetheless felt sorry for him now. "Long way around," he commented to nobody in particular; "might be fifty miles further."

"I didn't ask you!" Pryor snapped, and was immediately sorry. He strode off into the darkness, feeling like a spanked schoolboy.

By the Lord Harry, he was thinking, if he had that Laban in his command for just one week! *Just one week!* The trouble was, Hank Laban was a civilian employee and able to quit whenever he liked; and as Pryor had been given to understand before this, he was inclined to do just that on the slightest provocation. And Colonel Webb had assured Pryor only a week before that such men were hard to get.

Later, after Laban had disappeared to his blankets somewhere out in the dark, Frank Paddock explained to Pryor: "There aren't many trails in this country, Eden,

and Laban knows them. There are very few men who
do. We need him very badly."

After that Paddock went to his bedroll and stretched
out. He was dead-tired, and every muscle ached. He was
confused as well, for now that he had gone too far to
turn back he was attacked by doubts. When he had
made his decision he had been positive it was the right
one, and he still told himself this was so. But what if he
was wrong? What if the post, so ill-defended, was attacked?

He sat bolt upright, and for a moment was in a state of
blind panic, on the verge of ordering the command to
return to the post. Then he fought back his fears, and
presently he lay down again.

Maybe he had been a fool to go. So why had he gone?
Was it really because he could trap Medicine Dog and
score a decisive victory? Or was it to settle once and for
all his situation with Denise? If Denise and Kilrone took
this opportunity to leave together ... But if they did
not?

He turned restlessly, unable to relax, driven to wake-
fulness by the ghosts of his fears and doubts.

He was right, he decided finally. They would not
attack the post. The major Indian force was here, lying
in wait for M Troop and Mellett.

At last he slept. The firelight flickered against the
rocks and on the faces of the sleeping men.

Miles away to the south, Barney Kilrone awakened
with a start. Only a faint glow from the stove illumi-
nated the office of the post commander, where he was.
In a corner, on a pallet, were Denise Paddock and Betty
Considine. Stella Rybolt lay against the inner wall, and
Hopkins and his wife not far away.

For several minutes Kilrone lay quietly, wondering
what it was that had wakened him.

And then he heard it again.

Somebody outside was digging, digging under the
wall, under the floor where he lay.

The sound was faint but unmistakable; it was a whispering sound of movement, and the rustle of dirt falling in a narrow space. Somebody was trying to undermine the back wall of Headquarters building.

Under*mine . . . mine!*

Explosives . . .

Swiftly, silently, he got to his feet.

Chapter 10

There was no sound inside the building, nor did Kilrone make any in his passage. Tiptoeing, he moved as one accustomed to a need for silence. The firelight from the grate of the stove gave a faint red glow in the room, showing here and there the face of a sleeper—child, woman, or man—each seeming to rest in the comfort of a dream.

For a moment Kilrone looked on them, careful not to fix his eyes long on any one of them, for such an intent look, he knew, seemed to have a way of making a sleeper awaken. He looked on them with gloom, for what lay before them in a few hours might be violence and death; some of these had seen violence and death before this, and might again if they survived. He could not promise anything, either for them or himself.

In the outer room Draper, one of the teamsters, sat reading a battered magazine. He was bearded and somewhat bald—a tough, strong man, and a veteran of several Indian fights. He sat near enough to the wall to hear anything stirring outside, and his rifle was close to his hand. He looked up when Kilrone came into the room. "Quiet so far," he said, "but that means nothing."

"There's something out back," Kilrone said. "I'm going to have a look."

"Guards just came in," Draper commented. "Gittin' near the time."

"All right. Watch for me."

Kilrone eased the door open, listened, and then was gone into the darkness. Draper stared at the closed door a moment, and picked up his magazine again. But he did not read; he simply held it in his hands, listening.

Kilrone had moved only a step after closing the door. The night was dark, overcast, and cool. After the stuffy atmosphere of the building the outside air felt wonderful. He took time to fill his lungs a time or two while he listened for movement.

Then he went to the corner of the building, cast a quick glance around the corner, then stepped past, careful not to let his clothing brush the wall. He wasted no time, but moved on cat feet to the further corner and peered around.

A man was crouched in the darkness at the foundation, working stealthily. But even as Kilrone saw him, the man got up swiftly and moved away, stringing something out behind him.

Kilrone waited, watching him slip into a ditch that drained runoff water away from the buildings and the parade ground, and then he waited a little longer. He saw the man move away, and he was lost in the darkness.

Kneeling where the man had been, Kilrone dug carefully into the loose earth. His hands found a box and a fuse leading from it. Gingerly, he lifted the box from it's hole. The cover was merely laid on, and he lifted it. Inside were three cans of black powder, blasting powder.

Placed as they had been, there was enough to have blasted a good-size hole in the back wall of the building, and to have stunned or killed anyone in the room. For an instant he crouched there, considering. Then, with the box under his left arm, his six-shooter in his right hand, he followed the fuse.

It ended beside a rock at the edge of the ditch. The idea was clear enough. Once the attack began, the fuse would be fired and the resulting explosion would come close to putting anybody inside the Headquarters building out of action.

How about the other buildings? There was little time, but they must be checked.

Who had done this? It was no Indian trick, he was sure of that; and the man he had seen, although he had seen no more than his bulk in the blackness, had been no Indian.

He knelt beside the rock and moved some of the stones where the fuse had been waiting for the match. Then he dug out a chunk of sod with his bowie knife and quickly dug further into the soft earth beneath. When he had hollowed out a hole there, he cut the fuse to six inches, replaced it, and buried the box in the bank, as carefully as he could in the darkness. The rest of the fuse he left as it had been, trailed out upon the ground.

He went first to the warehouse. The back wall was the likely place, but he found nothing there. Undoubtedly the ground had been too hard to dig there without making noise, for a path led right along that wall. On the far end, however, he found another box, this one containing only one can of powder. He followed it out and did the same thing as before.

Next he went to the hospital, but after searching for a few minutes he found nothing. By now it was growing light, and he did not dare to search any longer.

Draper was at the door to let him in. Kells and Hopkins were standing by, and Rudio was at the stove, making coffee.

Betty Considine was waiting for him. "Where would you like the children to be?" she asked "Over in the corner?"

"We'll pull that desk over and turn it on its side," he said, "and put the filing cabinet there, too. Drape what bedding you can spare over the desk and the chairs. I've seen a folded letter stop a spent bullet."

"I'd like to feed the stock," Kells suggested.

"Stay where you are. It's my guess you'd never make it. Anyway, they'll take the horses if they haven't already."

No doubt the Indians were waiting for just that sort of thing. Lying in wait, they could attack the force remaining inside with small risk to themselves.

The fire in the stoves—there was one in each room— had been built up. Outside, the sky was faintly gray; the shapes of the buildings were taking form. No lights appeared anywhere.

Men moved to each of the windows, where they crouched, waiting. Stella Rybolt took over serving coffee and preparing breakfast, and Rudio took up his rifle. No lights were lit. Stella Rybolt worked by the glow from the grate of her stove, and as the food was prepared, carried it to the men at the windows.

Under the low clouds of morning the parade ground looked gray and forbidding. The buildings, standing silent and unlighted, were bleak. Nothing stirred.

Betty brought coffee to Kilrone and sat down on the floor beside him "Are they out there?" she asked.

"You can bet on it."

She spoke softly then, that only he might hear. "Did you love her very much? Denise, I mean?"

He shrugged. "Who knows? It was Brittany, in the spring, and we both were young."

"I somehow thought it was Paris."

"Paris was in the fall . . . By that time we were older."

"You are cynical."

"No . . . just wise enough to know that all loves do not last out the summer. And many of them should not. Let that be a lesson to you, Daughter of the General."

"And when you saw her again she was married to Frank Paddock?"

"Yes . . . and I was courting a dancer from Vienna."

"Then why . . . ?"

"Somebody talked to Frank, and he believed there was more than there was. Apparently the idea became something of an obession with him."

"Kilrone?" Hopkins spoke from his window. "Something moving down there."

He got up and went to the window, but stayed well back where he could not easily be seen. Looking down the length of the parade ground, he at first saw nothing. And then he saw a slight stir of movement in the shadows near a barracks. One, then another.

"Hold your fire," he said; "so far they've done nothing." He went to the window that looked toward the warehouse across a few feet of intervening space. He opened the window and called, "McCracken?"

"There's about a dozen of them in the brush along the creek," McCracken answered.

"Well, hold your fire."

The post, which was usually stirring with soldiers and military activity by this time, was all dark and still. The Indians would have seen or smelled the smoke from the stoves, but nothing moved about the post buildings. They had waited and watched, planning their attack, but nothing happened. Now they had come to see.

One by one they appeared, disappeared, then appeared again. They walked a few steps, paused to listen and to look, then impelled by a curiosity that robbed them of caution, they came out further on the parade ground. Undoubtedly this was the culmination of several hours of waiting and listening, for it was a certain thing that the Indians had been out there for some time.

"Teale," Kilrone said, "you and Ryan keep a sharp watch. When that explosion goes off, somebody is going to jump and run. I don't want them to get away."

"What explosion?"

"Don't worry, Teale. There'll be one. Right out there in front of you." He explained quickly what he had done, and Teale grinned at him.

Kilrone knelt at the window. His mouth was dry and he kept wiping his palms on his pants. It was very still out there in the growing light. Two of the Indians had turned and were walking up the parade ground toward Headquarters. Another one was trying the door of a barracks, but the door had been locked. He went to the window, put his face against the glass, and peered in.

Every moment of delay, Kilrone was thinking, was a moment won, for it was a moment closer to the return of the troops. He could hear his own heart beating. Within the room, nobody stirred, or even seemed to breath.

"Just wait," he said aloud, "let them look around."

There were several Indians around the corral, picking up what they could use. The horses had been gone before daylight. Including his own. A man didn't have to have much in this country, but without a horse he had nothing at all.

The sky remained gray and sullen, and over the mountains the overcast had shrouded the peaks. The color of the trees was beginning to be clear now, a deeper green, more somber somehow.

How did a man feel when he was about to die, Kilrone wondered. And it might come to just that. Any Indians out there at all, meant that there would be several hundred.

"They'll burn me out," Hopkins remarked gloomily.

"You'll be alive," Kells said. "How about that?"

But would he? At least, he would have a fighting chance here, and so would his wife.

Betty was suddenly beside Kilrone. "Barney, where's Mary?"

"The Indian girl? I haven't seen her."

"They'll kill her, Barney."

Would they? One never knew about Indians. She had been one of them, but was no longer. Or had she gone back to them? Many an Indian had, returning to her own or his own people even after every opportunity to stay among the whites. And wild Indians had been known to treat such Indians as they would a white man . . . or worse.

"She's out, Barney. We've got to help her."

"How? We haven't seen her. And where would a man look?"

"She'd go to the sutler's store. She lived there, you know. She'd feel responsible, I am sure."

He looked down the length of the parade ground. It was about 500 feet to the sutler's store, and the parade ground measured slightly over half of that. He felt something grow cold within him. To walk down there under the guns of the Indians, and then to return with Mary Tall Singer—if, indeed, she was there. . . .

"Do you have any idea how much chance a man would have to make it?" he said.

"Not much," she admitted. "Maybe I should go."

"You'd have no chance at all," he said. "You wouldn't get halfway."

They stood silent, and he looked down the field and measured it in his mind with his strides. How many strides before a bullet struck? How long would they wait before striking? The Indian is a warrior, and a warrior respects the brave ... would they wait to see if a man could walk that distance disdaining the danger? Would they be curious enough to test his courage? And did he have the courage to make that walk?

How far was it? How many steps?

A slow lift of smoke came from the store's chimney. "She's there, then," Hopkins said. "She stayed to watch my goods."

"Or for some other reason," Kells said. "You're forgettin' she's an Injun."

Denise had come from the back of the building. "She is an Indian, but she is loyal to us, too. I would not want her to turn against her own people, but I would never doubt her loyalty to us."

"You don't know Injuns, ma'am. They have no loyalty for a white man ... or woman."

Kilrone continued to look down the parade ground and felt the devil rising in him. He knew it was a wild and crazy feeling, but the urge was there. It was a challenge. . . . Could he make it? Could any man? If he started and then showed the least hesitation, the least sign of fear ... Hell, they'd shoot him anyway. He wouldn't get ten feet. It was a fool idea, the sort of idea that could get a man killed. But there was a girl down there in that store, a girl the Indians might be likely to kill.

If he started, how long would he have before somebody got trigger-happy and started blasting? How long before somebody back in the ditch behind the building decided to light a fuse? Or would they check that fuse and find out what he had done?

Nobody said anything, but they were looking down the same stretch that he was, and every one of them was thinking of Mary Tall Singer, a girl who had tried to go the white man's way, and whom they had deserted. It would look that way, wouldn't it?

Kilrone got to his feet. He stood his rifle beside the window. "I'll go get her," he said.

"Don't be a fool!" Kells said, getting up.

"You boys stand pat," Kilrone said. "Don't start any shooting unless you have to." His hand was on the doorknob.

"Barney . . . Mr. Kilrone," Betty said, "don't."

He opened the door and stepped outside and began walking toward the sutler's store. He kept his eyes straight ahead, and as he walked he ran through his mind the words and tune of an old marching song. He knew the Indians were all around him, that they might at any moment decide to shoot, and that at any sign of hesitation they certainly would.

He knew they were moving out from the buildings onto the parade ground. One dashed his horse across in front of Kilrone, but he kept marching. Not far ahead of him now was the sutler's store, and when he was about fifty steps away, the door suddenly opened and Mary Tall Singer stood there, waiting for him.

He walked up to her. "I have come to take you with me," he said. "Will you come?"

She looked at him with dark, enigmatic eyes, then she walked down the steps. Coolly, he offered her his arm, and they started back up the parade ground. The distance seemed twice as far now. Suddenly half a dozen Indians on ponies raced across the field toward them. Kilrone walked straight on, looking neither to right nor left, and the Indians, whipped by within inches of them. Yet he went on, unflinching, the dark-haired girl at his side keeping pace. Again and again the Indians raced their horses at them, wheeling not a foot away.

Then all of a sudden an armed Indian stepped directly in front of Kilrone, lance drawn back, and Kilrone walked right straight at him, looking into the cold black eyes. The point of the lance touched his breast, and he moved it lightly aside with his left hand, brushing it away as he might have brushed a cobweb or a leaf in the forest.

Ahead of him Kilrone saw the door open a crack, the merest crack. It would not be long now. He felt cold and the hair on the back of his neck prickled; the muscles between his shoulder blades seemed to tighten with the expectation of a shot or an arrow. But still he kept on.

Suddenly, from behind the Headquarters building there came a tremendous explosion, an explosion followed by three quick, barking shots.

Kilrone turned sharply on the Indians behind him. "Inside!" he hissed to Mary Tall Singer. "Get in ... *quick!*"

An Indian threw a rifle to his shoulder and instantly Kilrone palmed his pistol and fired from the hip. The bullet smashed the Indian in the chest a split second before his own shot went off, but the rifle tilted with the bullet's impact and the Indian's shot sailed off into the air.

Kilrone backed to the door, holding his fire, and then all the Indians seemed to be shooting at once. From the time of the explosion until now was no more than a few seconds, but time had seemed to lag. Kilrone fired, saw an Indian stagger, and then he leaped backward. Stumbling over the step, he went through the door and it was slammed and barred behind him.

He went quickly through the room to the back. Teale looked at him, his eyes glinting with hard humor. "Well, well! That's more'n I'd have done for an Injun gal!"

Kilrone glanced at him. "Teale, you don't fool me a bit. You'd have done it, and to hell with the price. I know your kind."

He gestured toward the ditch where he had planted the explosive. "What happened?"

"Plenty ... that explosion scared 'em more'n it hurt, but I reckon it did for one, maybe two of the Injuns ... and a white man tried to get away. He didn't make it."

"Good."

The shooting was general now. There were no Indians in sight, however. All were skillful fighters, and would not waste themselves in any useless effort. They wanted victory, but they meant to win it without too great a cost.

Kilrone made the rounds, looking out of the windows. The parade ground was empty. The Indian he had killed and at least one other killed or wounded had been carried away. So had any others who had been hurt. A shot came from a window of the nearest barracks, another from the corner of a building.

Beyond the parade ground and barracks clouds hung low around the mountain shoulders, and within the buildings was the smell of powder smoke. Now there was silence ... no targets, no Indians only stillness.

Kilrone could see the corral, and the horses were gone. Had he noticed that before? He had, he was sure, but he could not remember when. He knelt by the window, waiting, rifle in hand, but nothing stirred. Once a bird flew down and lighted on the parade ground, pecking at something in the dust. After a moment or two, taking alarm at something, it flew away.

They waited ... and waited ...

Half an hour went by ... an hour. The Indians were looting the barracks. Somewhere they heard the crash of glass, a window breaking.

Betty came with coffee and Kilrone sat down with his back to the wall and cupped it in his hands. Never had coffee tasted so good.

"That was wonderful," Betty said. "I mean, to go and get Mary."

"She had nerve. You know her hand on my arm never so much as trembled."

He had been doing some calculating. Unless Rybolt was shrewd, or shot with luck, he and his payroll escort were gone. Caught out in the open they wouldn't have a chance ... and the Indians would know they were coming.

What he was thinking about, however, was not so much Rybolt as Major Paddock, Captain Mellett, and the cavalry. They could not very well get back in less

than two days, and more likely it would be three ..
could they hold out that long here at the post?

But supposing they, too, had been attacked? Suppose
they had been wiped out? It would be weeks before
help could come from elsewhere, even if their predic-
ament was realized.

For the first time Kilrone began to think seriously of
escaping from the post.

Chapter 11

Throughout the morning the firing was sporadic, with little result on either side. Fire from the three buildings kept the Indians out of range most of the time, but not without cost. One child was cut, not badly, by flying glass, and in the warehouse Mendel was wounded.

He was standing at a broken window trying to get a shot, when an Indian hidden nearby put a bullet into his hip, turning him for the second shot, which entered near his spine and emerged near the belt buckle.

Early in the afternoon there was a sudden explosion on the hospital side ... a mine that Kilrone had not found, or one hidden since his exploration. The explosion knocked a hole in the wall of the building and killed Olson. For several minutes the Indians concentrated a hot fire on the hole and then tried a rush.

Two Indians fell from shots by Lahey and Ryerson, and the attack broke. One of the Indians dropped near the wall, and with a sudden rush got close enough to be out of range.

"We've got to get him," Ryerson said. "He's right alongside that hole. Any time we stop watching he can shoot right into us."

"You mean stick your head outside?" Lahey said. "You try it, Sarge. Not me."

Barney Kilrone crouched by the window. Somebody was moving around in one of the barracks about a hundred and fifty feet away. He could occasionally see a swift shadow against the window, and from time to time he heard a yell from Indians who were looting there.

He waited, biding his time. Then he saw the shadow again and lifted his rifle, taking a careful sight. He took up slack on the trigger, and felt the rifle leap in his hands as the shot went off. There was a crash of glass and the Indian fell backward through the window, one arm flailing wildly as he tried to catch the corner to break his fall.

Kilrone worked the lever on his gun and as the Indian hit the ground he fired into him. The Indian half rose, and then fell back.

"Watch him," Kilrone said to Ryan. "They'll try to get him away."

He went back, staying close to the floor because of the powder smoke in the room. Denise came to him when he entered the back room. "Are you all right, Barnes?"

"Where's Rybolt's wife?" he asked. "I want to talk to her."

"You sit here and I'll get some coffee. She'll be right over."

Stella Rybolt crawled over to him. He gestured toward the partition. "Sit down here with your back against that and have a rest. I want to talk to you." He took the coffee from Denise. "Tell me about your husband."

"What about him?"

"I never met him, and I'd like to know how he thinks. He must have talked a lot to you. I'm not promising anything, but I may try to get out and warn him."

"Don't try it, Mr. Kilrone. Gus would be the last to expect it."

"Tell me about him," he repeated.

"Well,"—she hesitated—"Gus is a soldier, first, last, and always. He's strict, but no martinet. He puts his duty ahead of everything." She turned her head to look hard at Kilrone. "That's why you shouldn't worry. His job is to protect that payroll and to bring back his men, as many of them alive and able as he can manage."

"Does he know Dave Sproul?"

She gave him a sharp look. "Now, how d' you mean that? Of course he knows him. I know him, too, and I'm not proud of it. Gus doesn't like him, if that's what you mean."

"Not exactly. Mrs. Rybolt, if Dave Sproul came riding up to him out there on the prairie, what would Gus do?"

"Do? I don't know what you mean. Talk to him, I guess. What else could he do?"

What else? She was right, of course. There was nothing else he could do, and that was the trouble, for the moment they stopped there would be danger. Kilrone could not believe that Sproul, being the man he was, would leave that payroll to chance.

If it vanished now it would be laid to an Indian attack, and any investigation would start with that in mind. But how would Dave Sproul manage it? And where?

The closer by, the better. He would need to be away that much less time from Hog Town and his alibi, and it would be in territory he knew well. But the risk was greater nearby in some ways, too. And who would he use? Some of his own men?

Yet why should Sproul go himself? He was, as Kilrone knew from bitter experience, a man more than careful to keep himself in the clear. It was not likely that he would himself ride out to stop Rybolt when he could have one of his men do it, someone known to Rybolt or the others, and whom they would greet without suspicion.

But Sproul would be close by . . . trust him to keep an eye on any gold. He would be close enough to watch, to oversee the job. There must be many suitable places along the route, but Sproul would choose a place reached by the payroll guard late in the afternoon, or at least after the noon halt. He would want them to have eaten, to have ridden off any immediate zest they may have had, and be tiring. Sitting sleepy in the saddle, expecting no danger, the guard would be glad of the short halt, and they would be sitting ducks for an ambush.

"What I mean is, would Gus be suspicious?"

"I don't know what you're gettin' at. No, he wouldn't be suspicious. Sproul's out prospecting a good bit. That is, Gus wouldn't be more suspicious than usual. Gus Rybolt isn't a very trusting man when he has charge of government property."

She looked at him thoughtfully. "Mr. Kilrone, what is it you're getting at?"

"Call me a fool, if you like, but I would not be surprised if, under the cover of this Indian fight, somebody doesn't try to get that payroll."

"You mean Dave Sproul? He'd never dare. He knows Gus. He wouldn't dare try it."

"I don't want to worry you, but I think Sproul would try if he thought he could get away with it. He wouldn't try though, unless he had what he believed to be a fool-proof plan."

She considered the idea. "I really don't know. As I said, Gus isn't trusting about government property, I know that, and he's very conscientious, but I really doubt that he'd suspect Dave Sproul of attempting a holdup."

Kilrone went on talking quietly with Stella Rybolt. She was a competent, rough-fibered woman and he had an idea that Gus Rybolt was the same—a good, sincere, and competent officer, but not one capable of matching cunning with Sproul. Yet Rybolt might be just the man to defeat Iron Dave. He might do it because of his very virtues, because he was tough, disciplined, and no gambler. He might just not give Sproul that inch of leeway he would need to pull it off.

Suddenly Stella Rybolt said, "I wish he did know. I just wish something would make him suspicious. Now you've got me worried."

"I didn't want to do that, Mrs. Rybolt. I wanted to get some idea of what to expect. If there's a chance, and if everything is going all right here, I might try to get down the trail to warn him."

"You mustn't try. You'd be killed."

"We'll see."

Kilrone went to the back window to relieve Teale for a spot of rest. As he watched out the window, he was trying to picture the route that Rybolt would follow to reach the post. He would be careful, but would not really be expecting trouble. Any white man he met would probably be considered a bearer of news, and Rybolt would certainly want information from him.

Sproul would choose a spot where the payroll guard would be out in the open, but where there would be concealment for the attacking party, and concealment for himself as well. For after due thought, Kilrone did not believe Sproul would approach the party himself. There was even the chance that the bearer of news would know nothing of the plot, and might himself be marked for death.

Nothing stirred out back. When Teale returned, Kilrone moved on and relieved another of the men, and so through the long, slow day he worked his way around the building, checking all the windows, relieving each of the men in turn.

In the hospital, the hole had been partly blocked up by overturning a table across it and piling furniture and cases behind it, but the wounded Indian was still there against the wall just outside the hole, and there was no way to get at him. As long as he remained there he meant danger to them.

Far down the parade ground an Indian showed near the sutler's store. There was a crash of glass, and then a smashing of wood. Hopkins swore. "There goes my business," he said gloomily, "and I never cheated an Indian in my life!"

The Indian showed again, and Hopkins took a long time sighting before he squeezed off his shot. The brave jumped as if stung, then disappeared around the corner of the building. "Good shot," Ryan said.

In mid-afternoon a ricocheting bullet scratched Draper, drawing blood but doing no real damage.

Within the buildings they waited for the night, waited in fear and apprehension. More Indians have arrived ... Kilrone figured there were at least four hundred now. Just before sundown the sutler's store burst into flames, lighting the clouded sky with weird effect.

Kilrone detailed men to get rest, tried to catch a cat nap himself. Tonight would tell the story. He tried to be matter-of-fact about it, but when he thought of the

women and children he could not be. And his mind
would not let him forget Rybolt, riding surely and steadily into an ambush. He thought of what could be done if
he could somehow get Rybolt and those six men here,
seven tough, competent, experienced soldiers. It might
make all the difference. And with Rybolt to take command, he himself could ride for Mellett or Paddock, or
both.

If the defenders survived the night ... if he himself
survived it ...

Captain Charles Mellett led his troop across the junction of the Owyhee and Battle Creek, and north to camp
near the head of Deep Creek. The Owyhee Range lay to
the west and north of him, the forest-clad slopes towering fifteen hundred feet higher than his camp.

From where he was now encamped, the quickest way
he knew of to the rendezvous on the North Fork was up
Castle Creek and it followed a route roughly parallel to
Squaw Creek. There was an old trail, often used by the
Bannocks and Utes, that led over the mountain, about
two miles east of Squaw.

"Doctor," he said, indicating the rough sketch he was
drawing on the ground, "our destination lies there. The
quickest route lies right over there"—he pointed toward
the northwest—"but I'm not going to take it."

"What's the problem?"

"It's too easy. If there are Indians around, they'd be
apt to know we're coming along. We know they're keeping up with us ... we lost a man the other night. So I
am sure they are somewhere over in the mountains
waiting for us. We'll make a feint in that direction, and
then cut around to the east and back."

"Sir?"

Mellett turned to see Keith standing at attention.
"What is it, Keith?"

"This, sir." Keith held out a hunting knife in a scab-
bard. "I just took it off an Indian."

"You've captured one?"

"Well, not exactly. He wasn't about to be took, and

when I saw him wearin' this, I didn't try too hard to take him."

"What about the knife, Keith?"

"That was Lister's knife, sir. Lister of I Troop."

Mellett turned the knife in his hands. Now that Keith mentioned it, he remembered the knife. Lister had often spoken of it, saying it was all he had salvaged from that government claim back in Kansas. If this was Lister's knife, then Lister must be dead; and if Lister was dead, what about I Troop?

"Sir, that there knife wasn't all. That Injun was wearin' Sergeant Bill Jordan's coat. I didn't fetch it along. It—it was somewhat bloody, sir."

"You're sure it was his?"

"Yes, sir. I watched him sew those chevrons on it with my own eyes. I'd know that work anywheres."

Charles Mellett got to his feet, his face gray with shock. If Jordan and Lister were dead, it was probable that Colonel Webb's I Troop had been hard hit, possibly massacred. It was unlikely that the Indians would have been able to strip Jordan's coat from his body unless they had caught him out alone and killed him, or unless the command had been wiped out . . . and Webb would not be likely to send Jordan scouting. Lister, yes, but not Jordan; he was too valuable to the command. He had to realize that the troop might have been wiped out.

"Charlie," Hanlon said, "do we dare move up there tonight? Some of those men may need me."

Keith was still waiting. Mellett turned to him. "Keith, go send Sergeant Dunivant to me. Meanwhile you get some rest. We'll be moving out before morning."

When Dunivant came up through the darkness, Mellett said to him, "Sergeant, let the men get some sleep. No fires. It is now eight o'clock. We will break camp and move out at two in the morning." He paused a moment. "I suppose you have talked to Keith?"

"Yes, sir. I saw the Indian, sir."

"You think that was Jordan's coat?"

"I know it was, sir."

"Then we can assume that Colonel Webb's command

has run into bad trouble. We can also assume there will be Indians waiting for us somewhere up ahead. I would suggest you pass the word along, Sergeant."

"How far to North Fork?" Hanlon asked.

"It's twenty miles or so by the most direct route," Mellett answered. "About eight miles farther the way we will go."

"Hell, isn't it? Men may be dying as we sit here."

Mellett nodded. "I know, but I'd risk my whole command going through that pass. If they're alive they're in action, you can bet on that, and they'll need every man I've got. The difference in time is about three or four hours, and less if we are lucky. I can't risk my own men for that difference. It isn't only the lives of my men, that I'm thinking of; it's a matter of military intelligence."

"You think the pass is a trap?"

"Your guess is as good as mine, Cart. All I know is that it could be, and if I were in Medicine Dog's place that's where I would wait."

"And by the other route?"

"We can still run into a fight, and probably will; but there's less chance of surprise, and a better field of fire."

Both men were silent then. They could smell the smoke of the dying fire, smothered with earth. And in the softness of the night they could smell the scent of the sagebrush and the pines. The clouds were breaking away, and here and there a star shone.

"You think they've had it, don't you, Charlie?" Hanlon asked.

Mellett considered the question. "I am afraid so, Cart. Jordan was Webb's strong right hand, and Whitman's too. He wouldn't be far from them, in any case. Besides," he added, "Jordan's coat and Lister's knife were found on one Indian. That implies there was loot enough for all . . . at least, it does to me."

At two in the morning the troop moved out. At thirty minutes past four they watered and took a break on Pole Creek. Ahead of them were three miles or so of wooded terrain, with towering cliffs on the east—one of the worst stretches they would encounter.

"I don't think we're fooling anybody now," Mellett commented to Hanlon. "It's my guess the Bannocks waited for a while, and when we didn't show they sent out a scouting party. We may run into Indians up ahead, but we're not going to waste time. We will go right on through."

Day was breaking when they came down out of the wooded stretch. The cliffs on the east held back the sun, but the crests were golden and red with the dawn's first light. The troop moved down the canyon at a good pace, the trail smooth before them, and every trooper rode with his rifle in his hand.

Keith rode out ahead, scouting the terrain. Suddenly he wheeled his horse and came back. "Captain, sir, a dead horse up ahead—a cavalry horse."

The column advanced slowly. The western side of the mountain was bright near the top; the sky above was blue, with a white cloud floating. They saw the dead horse lying there with blood on the saddle. It was Captain Whitman's horse.

Hanlon looked down at the saddle and the blood on the horse's flank. "Mellett, the man who rode that horse is no longer alive. No man could lose so much blood and live."

Keith had pushed on. He rode erect in the saddle, his rifle held ready, his eyes swinging from side to side, scanning everything, missing nothing. Again he drew up suddenly. "Captain, sir, I—"

They were there, the men of I Troop, lying in the awkward postures of death, struck down where they had been attacked, a small cluster of bodies together where they had fought in a last futile stand. They had scored, for blood was on the rocks from which the attackers had struck.

It had been neatly done, not in the most dangerous place, where the soldiers would have ridden with care, but where the open ground began to widen out and seemed to offer no hiding place, where the soldiers would have begun to relax. If, indeed, they had suspected anything.

"Dunivant, detail pickets and a burial detail," said Mellett.

"Sir?" said Keith.

"What is it?"

"I'd like the Captain's permission to scout around a bit."

"What is it, Keith?" Mellett repeated. "You know Indians, and there's something about this that bothers you. What is it?"

"The same thing that's bothering the Captain, sir. They did not take time to mutilate the dead. And they took no prisoners. They didn't even finish stripping all the bodies."

"So?"

"They were in a hell of a hurry to get away, sir."

"Go ahead . . . but be careful."

Keith wheeled his horse and rode away, Mellett looking after him as he rode off.

"That's a good man, Charlie," said Hanlon. "We could use a few more like him."

"He's a good soldier," Mellett agreed. "God forbid that he'd be anything else. I have watched him. He is not a man who would want to inflict pain on anything or anybody, not pain as such, but he's simply and purely a hunter, a man whose world is black and white, for and against, and no middle ground. War is his job, and he carries it out to perfection. You don't find many like him, but they're good to have on your side."

"And in peacetime?"

Mellett shrugged. "He would probably be quietly skillful at whatever he did, and law-abiding to the nth degree . . . up to a point. Beyond that point, an extremely dangerous man."

"He was getting at something. What was it?"

The sun had crept down the canyon wall. The burial detail, in their shirt-sleeves, were beginning to sweat. It would be a hot day, and humid following the rain.

"He has an instinct, Cart. I could see it bothering him all the while. Something about this venture was all wrong, wrong from the beginning. Webb was worried about it, too, which was his major reason for taking command."

"What did Keith mean about them getting away in such a hurry they didn't finish looting the bodies?"

"He believes this was a diversion, Cart, and the reason those Indians got the hell out of here so fast was for fear they'd be too late for something happening elsewhere."

"You mean ... back at the post?"

"That's what I'm afraid of."

Mellett waited, watching the burial party, but his eyes kept searching the mountainside, the valley ahead, everything within sight. He was sure in his own mind of what Keith would find: that the attacking party had been a relatively small one, and that the main body of the Indians were elsewhere. Thank God, Paddock was back at the post.

Yet as he waited a disturbing thought crept into his mind. This diversion had been skillfully planned. The Indian was quite a careful and cunning tactician, but he had never heard of an Indian planting the idea in the minds of the military that a dealer in rifles for Indians was to be in the field, in such and such an area.

For arms had been appearing—very fine rifles, in fact, and of the latest manufacture. The army was eager to stop that supply of weapons, and when the hint came to Webb—just how not even Mellett knew—he acted at once.

Webb had moved out with a patrol, with Mellett to follow and effect a junction on North Fork. His was actually a supporting force, planned to awe the Indians from any resistance.

Whoever had planted that idea had known just what Webb would be likely to do, and the area where the arms dealer was supposed to be was sufficiently far from the post.

"I never heard of an Indian planning like that, Charlie. They have brains enough, but they just don't think that way."

Mellet nodded. "We will go on through to the rendezvous. If anybody survived, that's where they'll be. I counted only fourteen bodies."

"We found another one," Dunivant said. "We just found Ryan. He was up in the rocks there, with two rifles and a pistol."

"Dead?"

"Yes, sir. He made a fight of it, sir. We counted six bullet holes, and he died up there after they left, because he was still dressed and they hadn't taken his guns. I guess they knew he was in a bad way and preferred to leave him to dying trying to kill him quicker."

"Good man, that."

"He was hit hard before he got up there. That's how we found him—by the trail of blood he left on the rocks. I counted fifty-nine cartridge shells up there ... fifty-nine! He may have killed as many as the whole command did."

Dunivant moved away and Mellett glanced over at Dr. Hanlon. "He's hoping Ryan killed a good number," he said, "but you never know unless you find the bodies. My guess is that it was a quick, sudden attack, and that the whole fight, except for Ryan up there in the rocks, didn't last more than a few minutes. The men weren't deployed as they would have been had there been any warning. I'd say several men went down with the first volley. Ryan made a stand, but wounded as he was he may not have done as much damage as we would like to believe."

When the burials were completed, Mellett mounted his men and rode on to Hurry Back Creek, where they made a halt for a brief nooning. Nobody was talking. The experience of burying friends had had a sobering effect.

When they reached the place of rendezvous in Pleasant Valley light was fading. Mellett led his troop in a quick sweep around the area, but in the vague light they could distinguish no tracks, and found no sign of Indians. They made camp beside the clear, cold stream and bedded down for the night.

Mellett had his boots off and was waiting for a last cup of coffee when he heard the sharp challenge of a sentry. He put down his cup and picked up his pistol, moving back from the fire.

He heard a sharp exclamation, then a babble of talk. Sergeant Dunivant came up to the fire. "Sir, Johnson's here. Johnson of I Troop."

Johnson, whose name had been something else back in the States, was a man of medium height, well set up, a good steady man of some education and refinement. How he came to be a soldier no one could guess. The men called him The Schoolmaster, and so he might have been.

Now he was tired, bloody, and haggard, but his uniform coat was buttoned and he still carried his rifle and canteen.

"Private Johnson reporting, sir. We didn't have a chance, Captain Mellett. They emptied half our saddles with the first volley it seemed like, and the Colonel was killed immediately. I made it into the rocks where Ryan was, but he was badly hurt and I wasn't. By that time the shooting was over. There was nothing I could do for him, and just before he died he urged me to get away. He was pretty soon gone, and I had to leave him there."

"How did it happen, Johnson?"

"They were under clumps of brush scattered along the trail. We took a hard volley from the edge of the trees, and then at least a dozen Indians seemed to come right up out of the ground around us. Jordan had been hit. I saw one Indian grab his horse by the bridle, and another jumped on the saddle behind him. The horse threw them both, and I was shooting. I—I don't think I hit anything, sir."

"You are lucky to be alive, Johnson. Sergeant, feed this man and let him change off between Evers, Little, and Drew. I think they're the lightest men in the troop."

"Sir?"

"Yes, Johnson?"

"Sir, there was firing off to the south this afternoon. It

may have been some distance off—the wind was right, and the air was clear."

"To the *south?*"

"Yes, sir. Whatever it was didn't last long. There was heavy firing for just a few minutes, and it ended abruptly."

When Johnson had gone, Mellett poked irritably at the fire. "Damn it, Cart! Damn it to hell!"

Hanlon smiled grimly. "That's no language for an officer and a gentleman, Charlie."

"That firing ... do you suppose that could have been Paddock?"

Hanlon was arranging his bed on the grass. He turned sharply. "*Paddock?* My God!"

Chapter 12

The Indians seemed to be waiting for something or somebody. Was it for darkness only? Or was it for the arrival of some one?

Mary Tall Singer was helping Denise change the dressing on the wound of the child cut by flying glass.

"What are they waiting for?" Kilrone asked her.

She did not reply for a moment, then looked around at him with an oddly defiant expression. "They wait for Medicine Dog. He comes with many warriors."

He considered that. It was likely that the Dog had himself planned whatever action was to take place in the north, and that what she said was true. The Indians could move faster than the cavalry, for they had much less equipment and knew all the secret passes through the canyons. Undoubtedly some Indians would remain behind to carry on sporadic sniping attacks on the mounted columns or on their camps.

What if they managed to stampede the horses of the cavalry? It had been done more than once in the past, and the entire command might be set afoot, miles from the post.

When they attacked again it was with no sudden rush. It was, rather, with a steady movement along the two sides of the parade ground, coming up behind the buildings in an effort to get into easy firing range.

It was Ryerson who detected this. Scarcely able to stand after the long, tiring day, he was crouched near the window when he saw an Indian inside a building hitherto empty. A vague movement drew his attention to the roof of a barracks, and there was another Indian.

Carefully, he eased his rifle into position. "Get ready!" he whispered. "Here they come!"

He glimpsed the Indian on the roof again, fired, and missed. Instantly there was a smashing volley through the hole in the wall, some of the bullets cutting through the table and other furniture piled up against it; then came a blow with a wagon tongue, and the tongue drove clear through the wreckage and into the room. An Indian lunged, trying to break through, and Reinhardt clubbed him with a broken table-leg, crushing his skull.

The attack came from all sides. First a volley by every rifle in Indian hands, then a rush for the windows and the shelter of the walls close by.

Kilrone standing up inside a window, levered shot after shot, choosing his targets with care. Suddenly, far down the parade ground, a barracks burst into flame, and then another.

"Well," Teale said grimly, "if they're anywhere within sight they should see that!"

"They aren't." Hopkins' tone was bitter.

All at once there was a thunder of hoofs, and through the billowing smoke that blew across the parade ground came the charging herd of horses from the corral. Taken some time before, they must have been held somewhere close by; but now they came rushing down upon the Headquarters building as if to charge right through it.

"Watch it!" Kilrone shouted. "There'll be Indians behind them!"

And there were—at least forty of them.

The herd split as it neared the building, breaking away to escape crashing into the wall, and as they broke away the Indians appeared, clinging low down on their horses and firing under their necks, as was the Indian way. They too split and rode to left and right, dropping from their horses close by the walls. Lahey, firing from a window, killed one Indian, wounded another.

On the far side of Headquarters, Draper fired into the massed horses as they pressed between the buildings, killing one of the Indians. He was leaning out for a shot at another when a bullet caught him in the chest. He staggered back, coughing and spitting blood, then went to his knees. He died there, sagging slowly to the floor, and for minutes nobody could get to him because of the fire the attackers poured through the unguarded window.

Kells suffered a minor wound; Hopkins had a gun shot from his hand, leaving the hand numb to the wrist. Kilrone opened up with his six-shooters and cleared the window. An Indian, running forward, suddenly leaped from below the window sill and grabbed his shirt. Kilrone, striking down with a gun barrel, smashed the Indian across the collarbone, missing his skull, and the infuriated savage clung to him, dragging him over the sill.

Kells grabbed his ankles and hung on, while Kilrone, fighting wildly against the wounded Indian, who was now joined by another, jammed his gun muzzle against the Indian's belly and pulled the trigger.

The Indian jerked convulsively, but still clung, sagging to the ground, his fingers caught in a death grip on Kilrone's shirt. Kilrone, struggling fiercely to get away, felt rather than saw the other Indian pull back his knife for a thrust, and then heard a gun blast and the Indian tottered back, his face shot away.

He looked up and saw Betty Considine, her face white and strained, holding a shotgun. "Get in ... quick!" she cried. And then the shotgun let go its second barrel over his head.

Jerking himself free, he lunged for the window, and felt something smash against his boot heel just as he slid through the window and was pulled to safety. He hit the floor and rolled over, and started to get up as Betty Considine coolly thumbed shells into the twin barrels of the gun.

"Thanks," he said. "I thought they had me."

She flashed a quick smile, then went back to the room where the children were.

There was no respite now. More Indians had come up, and they seemed to have no shortage of ammunition. Powder smoke filled the room. The men inside moved from window to window, firing, coughing, firing again. Women caught up the emptied rifles and thumbed cartridges into them.

Kilrone reloaded his six-guns, caught up his rifle, and returned to a window. Darkness was falling now, weirdly lit by the blazing barracks. It would be no time at all until the flames reached the officers' quarters.

The idea of escape was remote. They were surrounded on all sides, and the fire was intense. Obviously, Medicine Dog had arrived and was driving for a quick victory.

Stella Rybolt caught Kilrone's arm and pointed out of the window. All the glass was gone from the windows, which here and there had been partly boarded up or covered by furniture piled in the open spaces. Over the top of this obstruction his eyes followed her finger.

On the slope of the mountain stood a long row of Indians, where the sun's reflected light picked them out sharply. In blankets and headdresses, they sat their horses and watched, like spectators at an arena.

"You take it from me," she shouted in his ear, to be heard above the din, "they're waiting to see how Medicine Dog works. If they think there's a chance, they'll join; if not, they'll pull out."

They had done the same thing a few years before at Adobe Walls, down in the Panhandle of Texas. Some fifteen hundred Indians were reported to have stood watching to see what Quanah Parker would do.

How could they escape even if they wished? And how dare they leave the rifles and ammunition to the Indians? It would mean the death of hundreds of innocent people if those rifles fell into the hands of Medicine Dog and his Indian followers.

The attack suddenly broke. There were a few scattered shots, then quiet.

Kilrone thought of the little group of defenders. Mendel was badly wounded, Olson and Draper were dead. Kells had a scratch, Ryerson was ill. Their force had suffered badly, and there would be another attack at any time, he knew.

How many such attacks could they stand? Above all,

how many Indians had taken shelter close to the walls?

The women came now with coffee and thick slabs of bread. Slowly the smoke began to drift from the rooms. In a way, they had been lucky so far, but they could not expect such luck to continue.

Kilrone sank to the floor and checked his guns. All were loaded, all in working order. He accepted the coffee as it was brought to him, taking it from the hands of Denise, who dropped to her knees beside him.

"Where do you think they are, Barnes?"

"I don't know—headed this way, I hope."

"Do you think they've had a fight?"

He considered that. "Not much of a one, I'd guess. I think this is the main fight, right here. The hell of it is, a man can die just as easily in a minor fight."

Kells, his wound bandaged, was stretched out on the floor resting. Teale was slumped against the wall, half asleep. Battle took a dreadful toll of a man's strength, and the wise ones learned to sleep when and where they could—those who could were the lucky ones.

Nobody tried to do anything to repair damage done to their defenses, for everyone was exhausted.

The door of Headquarters was sagging, shot into fragments. It had been partly replaced by the door from the outer office to the commandant's office, which had been placed on its side, covering half of the space.

The clouds that had covered the sky earlier were now gone and the stars were out. The fires were dying down, but here and there among the ruins of the barracks that had burned, tiny flickering flames still ate hungrily at what remained of timbers. Some of the barracks still stood—one half burned, was only a shell, gaping to the sky.

Kilrone thought of Sproul. There had been no sign of conflict from Hog Town. No lights showed there, and all was still. No doubt the Indians had been told to leave Sproul's place alone. Kilrone had no evidence, but he knew Sproul was in this somehow. Those explosions had been set by a white man—perhaps by a renegade, but it was equally possible that it was by one of Sproul's men.

They might try that again. He thought of it, and knew it was likely, but there was nothing to be done except to try and spot any man carrying a package and trying to get at the walls. Maybe he was already there, maybe he had arrived with the stampeding horses and the Indians that followed. But Kilrone thought not. The man who set those mines was no gambler; he believed in safety first. He would watch his chance, move in, then get away quickly.

Kilrone stretched out his tired legs, and worked the fingers of his gun hand.

"I wish Frank understood about us," he said to Denise. "He's a good man."

She nodded, twisting her hands in her lap. "Nothing I could do would ever make him believe it," she said. "I tried."

His thoughts turned to Betty Considine. He remembered her face when she had shot that Indian. There had been an unexpected fierceness in her eyes. He smiled a little at the thought, remembering a line from an old story about a woman fit to bear a race of warriors ... well, she was the kind.

How much damage had they done, he wondered. Not so much as they hoped, he was sure, for it had always been so in battles between the Indian and the white man. The latter was inclined to exaggerate the number killed. The Indian had a way of vanishing when shot at, and many a white man who believed he had killed an Indian had not even scratched him.

After a bit he got to his feet and prowled the building like a caged animal, checking each window and each of the people in turn. From the end window of the building, he called across to Ryerson in the hospital. It was Lahey who answered.

"The Sarge is about done in," he said. "He's used up. He fell asleep as soon as he crawled to his bed, but he was right in there, throwin' lead with the best of us."

"Can you stick it?"

"Seems like. One more time, anyway."

"Lahey, you and Reinhardt get what medicines and

bandages together you can handle. We may have to abandon that building."

Then from the window nearest the warehouse, he called across a distance of scarcely twelve feet. If any of the buildings had to be held, it was the warehouse, but getting the children and women across the intervening space would be a very dangerous thing to try.

"McCracken," he said, when the man had appeared, "how are you over there?"

"We're all right. Not that we couldn't use another man. Mendel's in bad shape, and no use to us."

Kilrone turned his head slightly. "Ryan, come here." When the teamster was beside him at the window, he said, "They need help over there. Want to chance it?"

Ryan studied the windows, and the space between. He touched his tongue to his dry lips. "Sure, I'll try."

Kilrone turned again. "Teale, you and Rudio get to the front windows. Give Ryan some cover when he crosses. Don't shoot unless you see somebody aiming this way. I'd like to get him across without drawing their attention."

He was thinking of the women and children. Once the Indians suspected they might attempt that passage across, they would be alert for it, and would make the venture almost impossible.

Ryan climbed to the window sill, looked across, and dropped swiftly to the ground. Three fast steps and he had scrambled through, unseen.

It had been a reckless thing to do, and Kilrone knew it. He mopped the sweat from his face and sat down. They could hold out here only a little longer; and the window on the side toward the hospital would be under heavy fire from the hospital as soon as the Bannocks took over that building. Moreover, there were Indians right under the walls, impossible to fire upon, and just waiting to leap through a window or to catch anybody who ventured outside. One person they might manage to get across, but any real stir of action would be sure to attract attention.

Betty came to him. "Barney, have you thought of the roof? There's a trap door."

"Is there one over there?"

"There is in all the buildings, in case of fire on the roof."

He considered that. With planks or joists they might bridge the gap, then lay doors or something across them. But twelve feet ... it was quite a distance. And it would have to be done at night.

He went back to the window next to the hospital and called in a low voice. This time it was Reinhardt who came to the window. Could they make it across to the warehouse, Kilrone asked.

Reinhardt hesitated, and when he replied it was in German. Kilrone, who knew enough of the language for a simple conversation, responded. There might be Indians between the buildings, but it would have to be chanced.

Reinhardt vanished from the window, and Lahey appeared. When Reinhardt returned he said, "The Sarge says to leave him. He doesn't think he can make it."

"He'll make it. Get him over."

Again the distance was twelve feet. Reinhardt climbed to the sill, a bundle on his back, a white bundle that he had covered with an army blanket. He dropped to the ground and walked swiftly across and was helped through the window.

Lahey followed, half carring Ryerson. They had brought their rifles and most of the ammunition they still had left.

Suddenly Betty was at Kilrone's side. "Barney," she said softly, "I didn't want to alarm the others, but there's somebody in the loft ... above the ceiling."

He stood very still. He could feel the coldness inside him. The Indians were on the roof, then, and some had come through the trap door and were crouched in the loft, waiting.

When the next attack started, they would drop through the trap door and be inside.

Chapter 13

How many were up there? He listened, tuning his ears to sounds from above, trying not to hear those about him. At first he heard nothing, then he sensed a faint stirring, no more than a rat might make. But he doubted if any rats were left up there after all the shooting, for rats had a way of seeking safety in time.

How many? Not more than four or five, probably—the Indians who had stayed against the walls after the last attack. He went over to where Ryerson lay, his face gray with weakness, his eyes hollow and shining with fever.

"Tim," Kilrone said quietly, "did you help build this place?"

"I had charge of the detail. Lieutenant Rybolt was in command of the operation."

"What's above us? Is there an attic?"

"Nothing you'd call that. There's about four feet of space up there. You see our ceiling . . . one-inch boards, nailed to two-by-fours. There's no floor in the attic, if you want to call it that. There's a slanting roof, with just enough pitch to drain it, and a parapet around the roof about two feet high."

"Keep your six-gun handy, Tim, there's somebody up there."

Moving swiftly, he lined up all the men who could stand, and spaced them three feet apart. In their places, to watch from the windows, he placed Denise, Betty, Stella Rybolt, Alice Dunivant, and Martha Whitman.

"At the word," he said to the men in a low voice, "fire into the ceiling. Take a step forward and fire again; another step, and another volley. We'll repeat in the other room. We may not get them all, but we'll make them uncomfortable up there."

111

The men were ready. In another instant Kilrone
spoke. "Fire!"

The smashing roar of the rifles was deafening in the
confined space. Each man took a step, fired; stepped,
and fired again. Then swiftly they moved to the other
room, and fired into the ceiling from there. Dust fell ...
there was a moment of silence, then a groan. From a
crack in the ceiling drops of blood trickled and fell.

There was a faint stir above them, and three rifles
centered on the spot and fired. A violent movement like
a kick followed, then a weakening struggle.

"Are we going up there?" Lahey asked.

"Not yet," Kilrone said. "I don't want to stick my head
through that trap door, and I don't think you do."

The powder smoke made their heads ache. They
crouched near the floor, letting it slowly find its way out
of the broken windows and door.

Headquarters was a shambles now, the windows and
door blocked with broken furniture, the floor littered
with empty shells. Broken boxes of ammunition lay
about, and in the corners stood the barrels of water, the
supply already much lowered.

Kilrone stretched out on the floor beside Ryerson and
Lahey. Reinhardt, Teale, and Rudio were actually
asleep, some distance away. Hopkins, Kells, and the
women stood guard at the windows.

He felt utter exhaustion. There was a dull, throbbing
ache in his head, complete weariness in every muscle. He
lay still, his eyes closed, trying to think.

He believed it was unlikely the Indians would try
again to enter through the roof. But somebody might
still be alive up there. This was probably so, and a live
Indian, especially a wounded one, was a dangerous Indian. Yet if they wished to escape, that was the way they
had to go.

He thought again of Gus Rybolt, headed this way and
not far off now, riding forward unsuspectingly with his
guard of six men. Iron Dave Sproul himself or some
trusted envoy could meet the detail in a likely spot for
an ambush. Kilrone felt quite sure that Sproul would

send somebody else, some expendable man, and let him be killed along with the others. He would use Indians, for they would prefer the rifles he had to the money in the wagon.

The chances were the man would be sent to warn Rybolt. Sent to a specific place where there would be an excuse for him to wait and not ride on. That would mean a cross-place that offered concealment for a good body of Indians; a chance for one quick, smashing volley, with several guns aimed at each man. The whole thing could be over in a matter of minutes, Rybolt and his guard massacred, Sproul's messenger dead, or if he did get away, only able to say that he had been sent there to warn Rybolt.

The more Kilrone thought of it, the more he believed this was what would happen. He hoped he was wrong, but he could not make himself believe it.

And how long before help would arrive here at the post? There was no calculating on that. If they started back at once ... if they took a leisurely or a hurried pace ... if they were not attacked themselves ...

It would be one day more ... two days ... And when they arrived there would still be four or more Indians for every white soldier.

But Paddock would be sober; and sober, he was a good soldier. And Mellett would be there, a fighting veteran who knew what to do and when to do it.

He was dead-tired, weary in every part of his body. And Barnes Kilrone, ex-officer in the Army of the United States, thinking of these things, fell asleep at last.

Betty came to him with a blanket and stretched it over him. Denise Paddock looked at her and smiled wanly. "He is a good man, Betty, one of the best. A good man and a gentleman."

Betty looked down at him soberly. "I think so," she said, "but I don't think he has even noticed me."

"Don't be foolish! Barnes Kilrone never missed seeing a pretty woman in his life. Particularly," Denise added, "if she had good legs, and yours are beautiful."

Betty flushed. "I don't think he knows I'm alive," she said.

"He's been rather busy," Denise said dryly; "give him time." She looked over at Kilrone. "This is his life, you know. I know of no man so trained and conditioned for fighting. I mean mentally conditioned. Frank himself has often said that. I think one of the reasons why he believes I still love Barnes is because he admires him so much. He said he never knew a man with such an immediate and instinctive grasp of a battle situation."

Alice Dunivant came up to them. "Mrs. Paddock," she said, "please get some rest. I can take care of Tim."

Betty glanced around, suddenly remembering the Indian girl.

Mary Tall Singer sat huddled in a corner, a blanket over her head. She sat very still, staring at the floor. Her features were dimly visible in the vague light from the shielded kerosene lantern on the floor. Betty remembered then that she had neither moved nor spoken since being brought to Headquarters by Kilrone. The thought worried her. Yet these were her people who were out there, and some of them had died up there in the loft.

It was not a good thing to think about. And Mary must now be wondering where she belonged—in here with her adopted people, or out there with the Indians.

When Denise had gone to lie down, Alice Dunivant came over to stand beside Betty. It was very quiet now. No sound or movement came from above. Alice kept looking up at the ceiling. "I wonder if any of them are still alive?" she said. "It's horrible to think of them up there dead or dying."

"It would be worse to think of them down here ... alive," Betty replied shortly. "That would be the last of us."

"I know. I wonder how he thought of it. I mean, shooting through the ceiling like that. You would think a board would stop a bullet."

"One of these rifles or pistols will easily shoot through boards like that. I have heard Uncle Carter talking about it."

Barney Kilrone slept for two hours. A struggle at the door awakened him—a struggle, followed by a shot.

He lunged to his feet. Kells was fighting with two Indians who were forcing their way through the door. At that moment there was an explosion in the inner room. Kilrone palmed his gun and fired, his bullet smashing one of the Indians back into the darkness from which he had come. Kells fell, and the other Indian leaped past him and into the room. In an instant the doorway was filled with them.

The Indian who had leaped into the room, a warrior of powerful build, had grabbed Betty as she came running from the other room and spun her toward him. From the corner of his eye Kilrone saw that, but he had no time to act on that, for he had opened up with his six-shooter on the packed mass, struggling to get into the room.

Teale, who also had been sleeping, lunged in, swinging his clubbed rifle. The butt struck an Indian on the skull, and Teale, grasping the rifle with both hands, waded in, striking first with one end, then the other. Kilrone, shoving his empty gun into its holster, whipped his bowie knife from its sheath and closed with the nearest Indian. Behind him he heard a scream ... he dared not turn. If once the Indians broke through this door the battle would be lost. They would all be dead within minutes, including the women and children in the other room.

Suddenly the attack broke. One last Indian at the door swung at him with a knife and Kilrone parried the blade with his own, then lunged, the knife's cutting edge up. It sank into the Indian's belly, and he ripped it upward, the keen, heavy blade cutting through the breastbone. The Indian fell forward and, grasping him by the hair, Kilrone pitched him back out of the door.

Swiftly, they repiled the broken door and broken furniture across the opening. Only then could Kilrone turn.

The Indian who had gotten into the room was dead. He lay sprawled on the floor, the back of his skull crushed.

"She did it," Betty said, indicating Mary Tall Singer. "He would have killed me."

The Indian girl had ripped the Indian's own tomahawk from his belt and struck him with it. She still held it now, looking down at the dead man. "I know him," she said. "He came often to my father's lodge."

"It was a brave thing you did," Kilrone said quietly, "a very brave thing."

Martha Whitman and Alice Dunivant were kneeling beside Kells. The teamster was in a bad way. A bullet had gone through his body and his skull had taken a wicked blow from a tomahawk or hand-axe.

Kilrone went from window to window. The hours of darkness grew fewer, and still he had not decided what to do. Did he dare make an attempt to break out to warn Rybolt of what was coming? Did Rybolt need the warning? Barring something unforeseen, Gus Rybolt would be coming into the likely ambush area within the next twelve hours.

Did he dare even think of leaving here when the defenders and their defenses were growing more and more battered? Every rifle would count. Yet he might get a messenger off from Rybolt to Paddock—something, anything, to speed him up.

He would need a horse. That meant getting one from the Indians; or better still, one from Hog Town. There should be horses there, for there had been no signs of fighting in that direction, and no flames.

But before he could think of leaving, they must move to the warehouse and carry on what fighting they had to do from there. His original idea of defending all three buildings had been good enough then, but it was no longer so. If they intended to protect the rifles and ammunition from Medicine Dog, they could only do it from the warehouse. And whatever was to be done must be done soon.

Kells and Ryerson were out of action, and in the warehouse Mendel was in as bad a state. Every few minutes a bullet smashed through one of the windows or the door and ricocheted across the room. So far they had done no damage.

He looked up at the trap door, wondering what the chances were. What if there was an Indian alive up there? An Indian with a breath of life in him never stopped fighting. Nonetheless, if the move was to be made it must be from roof to roof.

Teale came up to him. "Cap, if you're thinking what I think you're thinking, you better have another think."

"What do you mean?"

"The moon, Cap Kilrone, the moon. It'll be comin' up within the hour. Once that moon's in the sky, you ain't got a chance."

He was right, of course, and there was a good chance the Indians were waiting for that moon. They probably had plans. The Bannocks did not mind fighting at night—not Medicine Dog's men, at least.

"Denise, get Sergeant Ryerson and Kells ready. They will have to go first, then the children."

"Without their mothers?"

"No, they will have to go, too." He turned. "Reinhardt, are you a builder? I think I heard somebody say you'd been a carpenter?"

"Yes, sir. That's right."

Briefly, quickly, he explained. "Rudio, you take the door. Keep your eyes open all the time. Hopkins, you go to the back window again. Teale, you work around from window to window. Shoot at anything that moves out there."

There was a stepladder in the closet. Kilrone got it out, took his gun in his right hand, and went up the ladder. While the others waited tensely, he eased the trap door to one side. Nothing happened. He hesitated, feeling the cold sweat down his spine. When he stuck his head up there he might get a bullet through it. He glanced down at the upturned faces, showing faintly pale in the gloom. Teale had his rifle lifted, ready for a shot.

Kilrone hesitated a moment longer, then removed his

hat, put it on the point of his pistol and lifted it slowly. Nothing happened.

He knew suddenly that he'd made a mistake. If there was anyone up there they would be watching not only for his head to appear, but listening for the grate of his foot on the stepladder or for the creak of the ladder rung.

Again he started to lift the hat, and as he did so he let his boot slide off the rung and lift. Instantly a gun bellowed, his hat jerked on the gun muzzle, and in that same instant Teale fired and Kilrone went through the trap door with a lunge.

The Indian was no more then ten feet away, and as he started to rise the movement stirred against the ceiling and Teale fired again. There was a jerk and the thump of a heel, then a slow exhalation of breath ... and silence.

Through the trap to the roof Kilrone could see two stars, and a broad sky. Shielding the glow with his hand, he struck a match.

There were four Indians, all dead. He blew out the match, then eased himself through the trap roof. The air was fresh and cool. He lay still a moment, breathing deeply; then he slid along the roof to the parapet, gingerly lifting his head, expecting the concussion of a blow at any instant. All remained dark and still, with a few scattered clouds overhead and many stars.

Across the twelve-foot space, the roof of the warehouse seemed equally empty.

Was the sky already lighter from the moon? Or was that his imagination? Did they dare risk it?

In any event, there was little time left. The bodies of the four Indians were brought up and tumbled from the roof; the joists were ripped out and lowered into position to span the gap between the two buildings. Four joists were laid a few inches apart, with cross-pieces tied in place with rawhide string. The bridge they made was flimsy, and it was dangerous, but that was a chance they had to take. They worked swiftly, helped from time to time by one of the other men, and by the women. Well

within the hour they had brought the children one by
one to the roof-top.

"I will go first," Denise said. "It will be better if I try
it, and the children can come to me on the other side."

She got down on her hands and knees and crawled
across. After a moment, they sent the first child across,
with Martha Whitman close behind. The others followed
carefully, one by one.

Now the sky was growing faintly gray. There was
little time left.

"Get Ryerson and Kells," Kilrone said.

He had kept that till the last, knowing the risk there
would be in moving the two wounded men. It would be
a slow process, and the feeble bridge might even col-
lapse under them.

"How will you do it, Cap?" Ryerson asked. "I am a
heavy man."

"We'll slide you on a plank. We don't have a stretcher,
and the plank is narrow, but if you lie still and help to
balance yourself, I think we can do it."

And they did.

At the end, there were six of them remaining in the
Headquarters building.

"All right, Hopkins. You first."

"Look, Kilrone, I—"

"You first, I said. No nonsense now. There's no time to
waste."

Hopkins went, and they could watch him all the way
across. How had the Indians missed seeing them, Kilrone
wondered. They must be watching, and now it could be
only a matter of minutes ...

"Rudio, quickly now! Then Reinhardt, then Lahey."

"Saving me to last, Kilrone?" Teale grinned at him.
"Figure I'm the one you could lose best? The world's
better off without me, or something like that?"

"Hell, no! You're the man I want with me if we have to
make a fight of it." Lahey was already crawling out on
the makeshift bridge, close on Reinhardt's heels.

The Indians saw them then, and a dozen rifles fired at
once. Kilrone, on his knees on the roof behind the para-

pet, saw the dawn blossom with spots of fire from the rifles, and he shot quickly, firing at the flash. Teale was down beside him.

Out of the corner of his eye he saw that Rudio had made the roof, saw him wheel and open fire, saw his body jerk with the impact of bullets—and then saw him fall forward and slip slowly from sight behind the parapet.

Teale fired a quick shot, ran, and dropped to his knee, firing again a bit to the left of a brown shoulder he saw. Kilrone, behind their parapet, waited, hearing the ugly sound of ricocheting bullets and, against the wall below him, the thud of their strike.

He glanced over at Teale. "Think you could run over that?"

Teale grinned. "Ain't no other way, Kilrone. You with me?"

"You go first," Kilrone said. "I hope that thing doesn't fold up under you."

Teale re-loaded his rifle, took a look at the narrow bridge, and crouched, ready. In the growing light they could see that the outer joist had developed a long split. There was an obvious sag in the middle, which meant that one of the other joists might also be broken. It was likely that only the crawling movement of those who had gone before had saved the make-shift contrivance; for by crawling, their weight was stretched over a wider area and did not put so much strain on the bridge. But now it was no longer a matter of crawling. Their only chance was in running.

Teale braced himself, then suddenly he was moving. He went up in a charging lunge; one foot hit the top of the parapet and the other hit the bridge almost four feet out. Instantly a terrific cannonade of shooting broke out as the Bannocks tried to get him. He was running full-tilt now. His second stride carried him another four feet, but when his boot hit the bridge there was an ominous crack and the bridge broke under him. He caught the edge of the parapet ahead and threw himself over as hands reached to help him.

Barney Kilrone crouched alone on the roof. They had him now. Could he jump the twelve feet? Without the parapet, he was sure he could have done it, but with it there was no chance for a running start, which he would need.

Suddenly there was a yell, and he saw Reinhardt pointing. Down the parade ground was a mass of horses, at least two hundred of them, and with shrill yells and shots the Indians were starting them again, to repeat their charge of the previous day.

"Teale!" Kilrone shouted.

The ex-cowboy turned and he called across to him. "I'm going to warn Rybolt!" He called just loud enough for Teale to hear him, and he did.

Wheeling, Kilrone darted to the trap door and went down the ladder, and ran swiftly to the window that opened on the gap between the buildings. The horses were coming now, and behind them a hundred charging, yelling Indians.

Dropping his rifle, he crouched by the window. Going through the gap there would be a time when the horses would jam up. He had taken many a flying mount, and this would not be hard . . . if he was not seen.

They came with a rush, and he threw himself from the window at a big gray. He caught the mane, mounted, and slid off to the side, only one leg across the horse's back, Indian fashion.

The horse burst through on the other side and went charging in a mass toward the brush and the plains beyond, and as they hit the brush Kilrone rolled over on his horse's back and slapped him with his palm.

Had he been seen? There was no telling, and so many shots had been flying that he could not tell if any were aimed at him. The big gray was one horse in a mass of others.

Charging into the thicker brush, he guided the horse and suddenly turned at right angles, and instead of rushing straight ahead with the rest, he rode south, keeping the wall of brush between himself and the fighting Indians. Their eyes, though, were directed toward the fort, away from him.

Presently he slowed his pace. He felt for his pistol, and found he still had it. The thong was in place and the Colt rested solidly in its holster. About his waist was a cartridge belt, another was thrown over one shoulder and under an arm.

Rudio had been killed, he was sure of that, but there remained, so far as he knew, eight able men. With the arms, ammunition, food, and water in the warehouse, eight men should hold it for a while at least. In the meantime he might warn Rybolt, and then start one or two of his men after Paddock and Mellett and their troops . . . or he might go himself.

In the meanwhile, those left at the post would have to fight. It was up to them now.

He headed south at an easy canter. He had some thinking to do, for he had to decide where to try to intercept Rybolt and the wagons, and he had to do it without being seen.

Chapter 14

Three miles south of the post, Kilrone drew up in a small cluster of cottonwoods and rigged a hackamore from rawhide strings such as he had used in tying the makeshift bridge together. He allowed the horse a little water, talked quietly to him for a few minutes, then mounted and headed south.

The big gray horse liked to travel, and he held his pace well. From time to time he slowed of his own volition, and then resumed his canter.

The morning air was clear and bright, the sky almost cloudless. He saw no Indians, although there were plenty of tracks.

In the remote distance, he seemed to see, as a vague blue line, the Slumbering Hills, and among them, Awakening Peak. But his imagination was perhaps recognizing the hills where there were only low clouds.

Finally he stopped, dismounted, and leading the gray horse, walked on in the glorious morning. Puffs of dust rose from each step; a faint cool breeze off the rain-soaked Santa Rosas was pleasant. War and fighting seemed far away.

Had he been wrong to leave? He told himself he had done the right thing ... he was not even sure he could have gotten into the warehouse from below, and he could not allow Rybolt and his guard to ride unknowing into disaster.

Eight men should hold the post, he told himself again. Ryerson was able to command, even if unable to help much with the fighting. Teale, Lahey, Reinhardt, McCracken ... all of them were good men, and the warehouse was strongly built, well supplied.

After a period of walking, he mounted the gray horse and rode on.

How far away would Rybolt be? Where would they choose to ambush him? Medicine Dog's ambush of I Troop had been in the least obvious place, and it was likely the Indians would try to do the same sort of thing now. More important, if Iron Dave was close by, watching his stake in the game, but out of it, where would he be?

It had been scarcely daylight when Kilrone started, and by the time the sun was approaching its zenith he was drawing into the danger area. At any time now he would come within sight of the detail commanded by Rybolt, or within the range of the Indians waiting in ambush.

Cane Springs? He thought of it suddenly. There had been a stage station at Cane Springs. It was deserted now, had been deserted since the outbreak of trouble. But the location was one offering conditions similar to those of the place where I Troop had been massacred. There was the pass between two mountain ranges, the Santa Rosa and Bloody Run, and then the widening out from the pass into the valley. And there at the end of the Bloody Run Range was Cane Spring, a logical stop. A place for nooning or a night camp before going on up the valley.

It had to be the place. The army detachment would have had approximately ten miles of alertness while coming through the pass. With the chance of fresh water ahead and a stop, they would be relaxing, already thinking of the cool water that lay just ahead.

The air was clear, so clear there seemed to be no distance, but only space in which nothing moved but the gentle wind. And there was no sound but the walking of his horse, the creak of his saddle, the occasional jingle of his spurs.

On his left the Santa Rosas rose steeply, four thousand feet to the peaks. On his right the Quinn River Valley lay flat and empty, only the distant line of trees along the river showing green and lovely. Where he rode there was no real cover.

However, the horse he rode was gray. His own clothing was nondescript, with no color that would not blend into the surrounding terrain, just as his horse did. He would move a little further to the south.

He traveled more slowly now to keep down the dust, and kept off the trail as much as possible, staying among the occasional clumps of juniper and the thickest of the sagebrush. Anyone looking for someone to approach would be watching along the trail; the further he was from it the more likely he would be to go unseen. The watchers would be paying little attention to the northern trail, for the payroll detail under Lieutenant Gus Rybolt was approaching from the south. But with every yard he advanced, the greater his risk of being seen . . . and if seen, killed.

Barney Kilrone drew rein in the small shade of a cluster of junipers, removed his hat and wiped the sweatband. Somewhere ahead, if he was figuring correctly, would be anywhere from twenty to two hundred Indians. But the more he thought of it the more he believed the figure might be not much more than twenty.

Most of the Bannock braves would want to be present at the taking of the post, and here they would have the advantage of surprise. With luck, having only seven or eight men to shoot at, they could concentrate their fire, two or three men aiming at each soldier. After the first volley they would close in. It need take only minutes.

Standing in his stirrups, Kilrone looked along the slope of the mountains toward where the gap should be. The promontory of the Bloody Run Range was obvious; at the base of it, not yet visible, was the old stage station, unless it had been burned. To the left of it, where the Santa Rosas ended, was the gap where the pass opened into the valley.

Suppose the Indians decided to attack just as the wagon was entering the pass, rather than as it was leaving? If that was the case he would be too late. By this time no doubt the guard would have been massacred. What he had to do was to find a way to get into the pass and warn the payroll detail before they could be attacked.

He edged on along the mountain, using each bit of cover he could, yet knowing the time would come when he must be discovered, or must emerge into the open.

Suppose, though, he started now, rode out into the open, and cut across toward the stage station? Would the Indians risk revealing their ambush by firing on him or pursuing him? He dismounted and led his horse on up to Andorno Creek. There was a trickle of water in the bottom, and they both drank.

He looked across the gap. The plain was flat. No trees or brush, nothing but low-growing sagebrush, a few sparse desert plants. He would ride out in the open, and he would have to take his time, for to make a run for it would be to reveal his purpose. He must ride slowly, tiredly, looking for all the world like a drifting cowhand, riding south out of the country.

Wiping his mouth with the back of his hand, he looked across the heat-drenched, dusty flat. White and still it lay, a place of glaring sun, without shadow, without shelter. If they came after him out there he would be a gone gosling. Yet the more he thought about it, the better plan it seemed to be.

If he rode boldly but casually out on the flat they would think of him only as a rider headed for the old stage station at Cane Springs. If he tried going under cover along the mountain and was discovered, they would know he was trying to slip by them and warn the detail.

Yet what if he did get across the flat? He seemed to remember the rocks behind the stage station were broken up, and there might be a route through them or over the mountain into the pass.

"All right, horse," he said, cheerfully; "we take the chance." He pointed. "We're going right out across that."

The gray started willingly enough, but Kilrone held him back until the horse had decided to mope along as his new master seemed to wish.

He followed along the mountain for a little way, then swung out on the flat. He rode steadily, taking care not to look back or to seem in any way to be expecting trouble. A hundred yards ... two hundred ... his scalp prickled with the expectation of a bullet.

They might try an arrow, but they would have to come after him now, and would expect him to fire upon them; the sound of a shot would go echoing down that canyon, and that would warn the soldiers.

In the dust he saw a horse's tracks ... fresh tracks. Out here where the wind blew, how long could tracks hold their shape?

Somebody had ridden across this flat within the last few hours, somebody riding in the same direction in which he was heading. ... Who?

It was a shod horse, a horse with a good long stride ... a big horse, too. Dave Sproul? But he drove a buckboard. Would he drive one, though, on such an occasion as this, when he would not want his presence known?

Of course, the rider might be a complete stranger, somebody drifting down out of the Oregon-Idaho country to get away from the Indian trouble.

Kilrone was a good mile out on the flat now, and if there were Indians waiting at the mouth of the pass, they must have seen him by now. Occasionally he glanced toward the pass. He was angling that way, ever so little. Where were the Bannocks, he wondered. His best guess put them somewhere in the breaks along Chimney or Porcupine creeks.

Suddenly he saw the wagon. At first it was just a flash of sunlight on a rifle barrel, then a wagon-top. Instantly, he slapped the spurs to the gray and swung right into the mouth of the pass. The horse must have made about four fast jumps before Kilrone saw half a dozen Indians break from the bed of Tony Creek, dead ahead of him.

Barney Kilrone, gentleman adventurer, soldier, and cowhand, he was thinking, *here's where you buy it. Here's where you wash it out, every last bit of it, so make it pay.*

He went down the canyon toward the Indians at a dead run, and lifting his Colt, he slammed a shot. He did not expect to hit anything, but he did expect to alert the oncoming wagon.

At that moment he topped out on a rise and saw a rider approaching the wagon, and the wagon slowing to meet him, but two of the soldiers were up in their stirrups, staring toward Kilrone.

The Indians were on him. There was one riding far out, to cut off any attempted escape, and four coming right down the center at him. He suddenly slowed his horse and leaped to the ground. He stood there, wide-legged and braced, looked down the barrel of his gun, and, lifting it as the Indians swept in upon him, he fired right into the chest of the nearest one. A lance ripped through his shirt, something burned along his shoulder, and a horse knocked him sprawling. He came up shooting, and suddenly the afternoon was filled with the thunder of rifles.

The Indians came around on him, and he saw his gray horse off to one side. He fired again, saw an Indian jerk in the saddle, and he put another bullet where the first had gone. The Indians were on him again, and he threw himself down a grassy slope into a small gully, rolled over and came up, diving into the brush as a rider came down on him. He felt the lance tear through his pants leg and plunged through the brush, fighting his way out.

As he came up, he saw an Indian rounding the clump of brush with bow lifted, arrow pointed at him. He dropped an instant before the arrow left the bow, fired, missed, and fired again. He slid down a steep bank into the creek, where he stood knee-deep in the water and ejected a cartridge, fed another in, and scrambled into the brush just as a Bannock came downstream, hunting him.

He pulled back, a branch cracked, and the Indian turned and fired. He felt the bullet smash through the brush within inches of his skull, but he dared not fire. He had to make each shot count. He had managed to reload one chamber—were there two shots left—or only one?

The Indian was trying to force his horse up the bank, but it was unable to get a foothold. The Indian fired again, but although he was closer now, his horse's movement spoiled the shot. A gap showed in the bushes and Kilrone fired, saw the bullet smash blood from the warrior's cheek, and then he scrambled back as bullets came from other directions, stabbing into the brush after him. Lying flat, he ejected another cartridge and loaded, loaded another and another.

As he made his way through the brush, he saw a game trail wide enough for him and eased down it.

He paused again to eject a cartridge and load another chamber. Crawling on, he saw his gray horse thirty yards off, and left his cover on a run. The gray wheeled as if to run, and he called out to it. The big horse hesitated, and in that instant he reached it, grabbed the pommel, and left the ground in a leap, almost losing his grip on the gun as he swung astride.

A shot smashed behind him and he rode into the brush, turned at right angles, then went up the slope and out of the creek bed.

Before him, not fifty yards away, a horse was down, struggling in its harness; one soldier lay sprawled, and the others were firing, coolly and carefully.

With a yell he started toward them and saw a soldier lift his rifle to fire, saw Rybolt's hand drop to the man's shoulder, and then he drew up and slid to the ground. "Come to warn you!" he called. "The post is under attack, Paddock's gone north after Mellett!"

Dropping down, he scrambled to the dead or wounded soldier, grabbed his rifle, and stripped his cartridge pouch. He fired immediately, and then again. The Indians wheeled away, and for a time there was silence.

"Kilrone, isn't it?" Rybolt said. "I heard you were up here. What's happened?"

Crouching low, while the others dug with bayonets to throw up a wall of turf, he explained what had happened at the fort, and what he believed was happening here. "What happened to the white man who came to stop you?" he asked.

Rybolt pointed. "Out there." He saw the body, with the rusty hair, lying among the Indians who had been shot down on the first attack.

Kilrone sliced into the sod with his bowie knife and cut out a long rectangle of it. Quickly he cut others, hollowing out the ground beneath him, and piling them in place. Their position was not at all bad; the Indians had tried to catch them in the open, but they had also provided them with an excellent field of fire.

He continued to work until he had a protecting wall of sod; and now he lay quiet. He smelled gunpowder and blood, the stale sweat of his own body, and the cool earth where he lay. What would they do now? The initial attack had failed, at least a third of the attacking force seemed to be down—either dead or injured. Scattered shots struck near the soldiers, but they did not return the fire. Their rifles re-loaded and ready.

"How many do you think there are?" Kilrone asked.

"Thirty . . . no more than that." Rybolt answered, and looked around at him. "That shot of yours saved our bacon. Somebody saw the dust in the distance, and then that other rider showed up. That bothered me some, because your dust was back a little way, and I couldn't figure where this one came from. Then you shot, and we were all set for trouble when the Indians opened up on us."

After a moment he asked, "You saw Mrs. Rybolt?"

"Yes, I did, Lieutenant. When I left there she was in fine shape and doing the work of two people." He explained about the move to the warehouse.

"It's a good, solid building," Rybolt said. "I think it will hold."

It was very hot on the little knoll. They could hear the water in Porcupine Creek, directly before them. There had been no attempt to kill the horses; the one lying out there might have been hit by accident. It could be that Sproul planned to use them to haul away the gold, if he got it.

Where was Sproul? Was he still somewhere close by? Was he waiting at the stage station even now?

Chapter 15

Shadows gathered in the notches of the Bloody Run Hills. The horses were clustered together now under the bank of a small ravine near the wagon. Working with their knives and bayonets the troopers had dug out a trench leading to the ravine, and had snaked up some dead-falls and piled them into a parapet.

Gus Rybolt was a soldier, a veteran, a careful man. He allowed no resting time until their shelter was improved. The ravine was scarcely more than a notch in the earth leading down to the bank of the creek. It provided shelter for the horses and for three of the men, the others remaining in proximity to the wagon and the gold they protected.

Rybolt had been cool, efficient, aware of every possibility. Kilrone found a corner in the ravine where there was shade and shelter from the ricocheting bullets, and stretched out to rest.

Surprisingly, he slept. When he woke he listened to the silence a moment, then crawled over to where Rybolt was sipping coffee, unperturbed by the occasional bullet that whistled by overhead or smacked into the wall opposite.

"Coffee?" Rybolt said, and gestured toward the pot. "Spare cup yonder."

When Kilrone was seated beside him, Rybolt said, "Nobody is going to get this payroll without more of a fight than this. My idea is they'll quit."

It was Kilrone's idea too. Sproul had planned on a sudden surprise attack, a quick victory, the Indians then returning to their people at the post, and he himself driving the wagon away with its gold.

Only Kilrone's warning and Rybolt's alertness had

wrecked the plan. Rybolt had lost a man; but here he was, dug in securely, showing no disposition to be stampeded into any foolish action, and apparently ready to stand a siege.

"After dark," Kilrone said suddenly, "I'm going to try to get out of here. I want to check that stage station up at Cane Springs."

"Wait . . . play it safe. They'll be gone by tomorrow."

"Tonight," Kilrone said. "There's too much at stake."

The silence and the waiting brought on a brooding feeling. Suddenly he wanted to get away from it all. He wanted to get away from the fighting, away from northern Nevada, clear away from Denise and Frank Paddock and everything connected with them. Frank was the lucky one, having Denise. What good did it do a man to keep moving from place to place, and never a place of his own? Being around them had only intensified the feeling.

Of course he could not leave now. He owed it to too many soldiers he had known, and to too many Indians. And he had to get Dave Sproul. Whatever else happened, Sproul must be exposed, defeated, driven from the western frontier. Too many men had died because of him, both Indian and white.

After that he would ride out again, yet even as he told himself this was what he would do, he knew it meant only more riding. Somewhere, somehow he had missed the boat. He had traveled, and he had seen much of Europe and the United States, and he knew that here in this far-western land was all he wanted of home.

Well, not quite. It was all right to talk of riding free, of having a home wherever he hung his hat, but it did not work out that way. With all that far horizons had to offer, there was something that was missing. A man needed a woman . . . he needed someone to turn to in the night, someone to share things with, someone to whom he could say, "Look at that now!" So many times he had seen the beautiful when there were no other eyes to share it with; too many times he had wished to speak and to listen, and there had been only a horse and a lonely campfire.

He was no longer worried about Rybolt. The man was a good soldier, stern, but considerate of his men, alert for trouble—a man careful when care was needed. Rybolt was in a secure position, and it would take many more Indians than these to trouble him. And when the attack broke in the north, if it did, it was unlikely those Indians would come south. They would ride east and north toward the Bitterroots or the Beaverhead Mountains, and lose themselves there. A few might scatter into the Steen Mountain country.

Kilrone went to the gray horse, stripped off his gear and let him roll, then rubbed him down with handfuls of coarse grass. He let him drink from the trickle in the bottom of the ravine, then saddled him again.

There was only sporadic fire now. The Indians had lost their taste for it. They might make an attempt during the night, but more likely toward dawn ... if they were still around. This was not an easy position to attack. To approach from the ravine side was impossible, and on the other sides the charge must be uphill and in the open.

Kilrone drank coffee, chewed on some jerky, and waited for darkness.

Gus Rybolt came from the breastwork and dropped to his haunches beside him. "You riding out?"

"I'll have a look over at Cane Springs. If Sproul is around he'll be there."

"You're sure about him? I always knew he was a crook, but I never figured he'd be dealing with the Indians."

Before midnight, Kilrone led his horse from the ravine, shook hands with Rybolt, and then led the horse away, keeping to the side of the knoll to leave no outline against the sky. Every few steps he paused to listen, but the night sounds were normal ones, and when he was out at least fifty yards and had found no trouble, he turned at right angles and mounted the gray, riding toward Tony Creek.

He crossed the creek and paused again to listen. He heard only the sounds of small animals stirring, and the wind. Far off a coyote yapped irritably at the sky. Following the sandy bed of the stream, where water flowed only along one side, he rode on until he could smell the water at the springs and feel its coolness. He knew there were several good-size pools there much of the time, and the stage station lay just north of them.

Leaving the gray in a clump of brush, he went on up to the buildings. There was a long, low-roofed structure a shed, and a couple of pole corrals.

He waited for several minutes, feeling of the night. Overhead the stars were out and, his eyes being accustomed to the darkness, he could see well enough, except for the deepest shadows under the trees or near the station itself.

There were no horses in the corral, but he believed he detected a faint smell of smoke in the air. Moving with care, he crossed the yard and went along the side of the corral.

The place smelled of trouble. Hesitating at the corner of the corral, he listened again. The building seemed to be empty. The shuttered windows showed no light, but the door stood slightly ajar. As he started to step forward something slipped under his boot and he caught himself. Curious, he crouched, feeling about with his fingers.

Mud ... on the bottom of his boot.

Despite the rains of the past few days there was little mud anywhere around, for this was a dry, thirsty land that drank its water swiftly, or let it run off into the sandy washes that carried it into the creeks. The area around the stage station was hard and dry ... but there had been mud when he passed one of the small pools that lay behind him.

Gently his fingers searched the ground. Near the corral where the ground was softer, he found a track. His fingers traced it out ... a horse-shoe track; mud around the edges, mud still wet. He sat back on his heels.

If that mud had been dropped here as late as mid-afternoon it would now be dry, for the day had been hot; therefore whoever had left it there was likely to be in the vicinity. There was every chance that he had come to this place since sundown ... perhaps since darkness, for he might not have wished to be seen.

The track seemed to be smaller than that made by one of the big horses Sproul would ride . . . when he rode.

He felt around in the darkness, found a smear of partial tracks. The horse might have been tied here while the rider looked around inside.

Was he still here? It seemed doubtful, but it must have been late when he arrived. Who was he? And why had he come here?

If Barney Kilrone had learned one thing in his years, it was the necessity of waiting. Many troubles removed themselves if one merely waited; and it was invariably bad policy to be too hasty. If there was a man inside that building, he must move sooner or later; and if he moved he would probably make some sound.

Kilrone doubted the man would be Sproul, though it was possible. He waited while the moments passed, and when some time had gone by he heard a faint creak from inside the building. A settling of timbers, caused by changing temperature? A movement of some small animal? Not the latter, he was sure.

After a minute the sound came again. There was movement within the house.

Kilrone felt his heart beat with heavy emphasis. He took a deep breath, and waited again. There was no further sound, nothing to be seen. He desperately wanted to move. The back of his neck itched, and he wanted to dry his palms on his shirt.

Was that a movement near the window? Or was it his imagination?

The rifle he had taken from the dead soldier he had left with his horse. He carried only his pistol and knife. What lay ahead would be close work, if any.

Sproul? He had underrated the man before, and Sproul might have waited, wanting Kilrone, and sure that he would come.

Down the valley all was quiet. The Indians might be waiting until the hour before dawn, or they might have decided against a further attack. After all, for them the loot was small.

Suddenly something moved at the door. A man staggered into view, leaning against the door jamb for a moment. He seemed to cling there, then staggered into the open and fell to the ground.

Startled, Kilrone made a step forward, then stopped. The man lay face down on the ground in the open and in plain sight. It was a bright, still night, and the dark figure lay against the white hard-packed sand of the dooryard. In his right hand, flung out from his body, was a rifle.

For a long moment Kilrone held himself back. The man appeared to be hurt; perhaps he was dying.

Kilrone waited a minute, two minutes. He stepped out, moved into the shadow of the stable, and nothing happened. He moved closer, allowing himself to appear briefly in the lighter area, and still nothing happened. He went forward, stopped near the man and bent forward, peering down at him.

"What's wrong?" he asked. "What is it?"

The man groaned, and Kilrone took him by the shoulder with his left hand, about to turn him over. He started to turn him, and suddenly a derringer, clutched in the man's left hand, belched fire.

An instant before Kilrone's mind sensed the gleam of metal that was the gun, his hand was moving. Instinct trained so long, did not fail him now. Even before his mind could comprehend the trick, he was firing.

The derringer blasted in his face, something stung wickedly on his cheek. It was point-blank for both of them, but the man on the ground had trusted to that one close-up shot . . . and it missed.

Kilrone had let go the man's shoulder and shot into him three times before he could stop himself.

He backed off, his gun poised. He crouched, waiting. The man on the ground did not move for a moment, then a leg moved, a toe dug in, and the leg stretched out slowly.

Gun ready, Kilrone went up to the man and turned him over with his toe. It was the man who had been in the Empire that night, the man at the bar who had done nothing during the trouble.

Blood gleamed wet in the vague light, dark blood forming a pool beneath him. Kilrone kicked the fallen derringer aside and the man's eyes opened.

"Luck," he muttered, "you're shot with luck."

"Dave Sproul send you?"

"He'll get you. He always gets them."

"Not me. This time I'm going to get him. I'm going to beat him with my hands."

There was no reply. The dying man was breathing hoarsely. It was ugly to hear. "Like ... like to see ... " The man's eyes flared open. "I ... almost had you."

"It was a good try."

Barney Kilrone looked down at the man, wondering how much Sproul offered him. It could not have been much, and in any case it was not worth this. It never was worth it. Again he thought how foolish crime is. Here a man was dying ... for how much? Two hundred dollars? He had known them to die for less. No more women, no more bright mornings, no more gaiety and laughter ... all gone, thrown away, for this.

"Anybody you want me to notify?" he asked. "I'd write a letter."

The man's eyes opened again. His breathing was ragged and occasionally seemed almost to stop altogether. "Hell, no. Never had nobody ... squaw, one time." He lay there under the pure, still stars, and time seemed to stand still. Then he said clearly. "She was a good squaw ... I didn't deserve her."

"Well, I could write to somebody." There was no reply, and after a moment Kilrone said. "You got a name? I'll put it on the marker. There's somebody knew you ... somewhere. A man should leave some kind of a mark on the land."

"Poole," the man said. After a bit he added, "I was a scout for the Fifth Cavalry one time. I knew Injuns."

Another long minute went by, and then he opened his eyes again. "What you waitin' for?"

Kilrone squatted on his heels. "You tried to kill me, Poole, but no man ought to die alone ... not like this. I'll wait."

After another silence Poole said, "Thanks ... I won't be long."

Kilrone pushed his hat back on his head. It had been a warm day but it was cooler now. The coyote was talking again, and a nighthawk swooped and dipped in the sky.

Suddenly the dying man spoke. "Mag? *Mag!* Damn it, Mag, I ... "

And that was all.

Kilrone got to his feet, feeling no animosity for the man. "So there was somebody, after all," he muttered. "Or was that what he called the squaw?"

And then there was only the sound of a spade in the half light, a spade working, pausing, working. After that, a scratching on a board, the scratching of a knife.

Finally, retreating hoof-beats, dying away, and then only the coyote, calling into the night.

Chapter 16

Major Frank Paddock, sober, alert, and in command, brought his cavalry down from the hills at a good trot. He had pushed them hard, taking only a few breaks. Time for water and feed, a quick meal, and back in the saddle again. There was no time for sleep, and nobody wanted to sleep.

There were men in that command who had wives and children at the post. There were others who had no one, anywhere, but they were soldiers. They cussed the riding, the lack of sleep, and their officers, one by one. They cussed their officers and did it well, cussed them as Alexander's men had cussed, as the legionnaires of Rome had cussed, as Napoleon's men had sworn among themselves at their Little Corporal and his forced marches. They cussed them as good soldiers always had; and like good soldiers they fought.

They came down out of the hills near the post and they spread in a hard line and they came riding hard. Before their attack the Indians broke for their horses.

The Indian was never a fool: when a fight was over, he left. There was always another day. Of course, after this time there would be no other day, but that they could not guess. The red man had both courage and savvy; and his savvy told him now that there was no sense in fighting under these circumstances.

Like ghosts, they vanished into the night. There was no one trail; there were hundreds of trails, and a wise man does not try to follow so many. At one moment the Indians were fierce fighting men, moving in for a kill at this remote Alamo; then, like snow under a warm wind, they were gone. And with them went the dreams of Medicine Dog.

He had thought well, planned well, and his plan should have worked. Who would have believed so few men could fight so hard a battle? These men were warriors, too, good warriors. Medicine Dog had only respect for a good fighting man.

In the meantime he would ride east, he would ride very fast. He knew where there was an Indian agent who was a good man, and he would say, "Me Medicine Dog . . . good Indian."

He chuckled into the night. Oh, they would believe him, all right! They would pat him on the back, give him a blanket and a beef ration. Of course, the other Indians would know better, but the other Indians would not talk.

He had a good horse, a rifle, a pistol, and he knew where there were a few more horses nobody would be claiming now . . . He wished he had a watch—he had always wanted a big gold watch like that one Dave Sproul had. Maybe he could find one. He would be passing some lonely cabin somewhere . . . but that could wait.

Medicine Dog, the Indian Napoleon who stubbed his toe when he went against a handful of soldiers in an adobe warehouse, rode eastward. He would camp tonight where the horses were, in Paradise Valley.

They were standing outside the buildings when the troopers returned from the fighting—the women and the children and the surviving men.

Hopkins had a flesh wound in the shoulder. Ironically, with almost the last shot of the battle, Dawson had been killed. He had stood up to fire at the retreating Indians, and one of the braves, turning in his saddle, let go a random shot and the farrier fell across the window sill, dead.

Denise was not among those outside the warehouse. When the Indians fled she had gone to her own house. The place had been looted, but there was were some things left. She found a coffeepot and a small store of coffee the Indians had missed. She started the fire and put on the pot and began to straighten up the room.

Betty Considine came across the parade ground to her. "Can I do something?" she asked.

"No," Denise replied. "You'll think I am foolish, but I want to do this myself. And I want Frank to find me here when he comes in."

Betty hesitated a moment longer, looking at the shambles about her, and watching the way in which Denise was bringing order out of chaos. "You are lucky," she said at last. "You've somebody coming home to you."

"Dr. Hanlon will be coming back. I saw him ride through with the troops."

"Dr. Hanlon is my uncle, and I love him, but that was not what I meant."

Denise put a chair in place, looked ruefully at a table with a broken leg, and propped up the corner with a box.

"Betty, you're a fool if you let him get away," she said.

"Who?"

"You're in love with him," was the reply. "Don't think I have missed seeing that. And he's a good man—one of the very best."

"He's a drifter."

"Try him. I never knew a man who would appreciate a home as much. He's been long enough without one."

"I haven't seen him out there. He may have been killed." As she spoke something within her went cold and tight, and for the first time she knew fear. "He may not come back."

"He'll come back. He's that sort."

Betty Considine walked down the row of buildings to her uncle's quarters. Surprisingly, she found little damage there. Windows had been broken by stray bullets, but there had been no looting. To the Indians, Dr. Hanlon was a medicine man. He had treated Indians when they were injured with the same attention he had given the soldiers or the white civilians. Partly because of that and partly because of superstition, they had left his quarters alone, and all the strange bottles, instruments, and equipment that Dr. Hanlon kept in his home had not been touched.

Nor had the hospital been looted, except for blankets and food left there by the soldiers. The medicines and all the instruments here had also been left untouched.

Then she thought of Iron Dave Sproul.

She went to the door and shaded her eyes against the sun. The first man she saw was Teale. He had caught up a horse and was looking among a lot of debris for a saddle. Quickly she crossed the parade ground. "Mr. Teale," she called.

Startled at the unfamiliar title, he turned.

"Mr. Teale, I've got to find Mr. Kilrone."

"With all due respect, ma'am, you walk back to your house now, and you just stay there. These are rough times. If I see Kilrone I will tell him you're wishful to see him."

"That won't do. I want to see him before he goes to Hog Town."

Lahey came up, mounted and leading a spare horse. "McCracken's comin'," he said; "so are Ryan an' Reinhardt. There'll be more, too, when word gets around."

"Now, ma'am, I—"

"Don't say it, Mr. Teale. You're all going, I can see that. Well, I am going, too." She turned to Lahey. "Mr. Lahey, I will take that horse."

"I am sorry, ma'am. You can't have it. No lady goes to Hog Town . . . least of all, you."

"I demand that you give me that horse!"

"Sorry, ma'am." Lahey was firm. "I'll not do it."

"Well, then, you can tell me this: Has Mr. Kilrone gone there?"

"No, ma'am. Not that we know of."

"But you think he might?"

"Ma'am, I know he will, if he's in shape to fight. He's got him a good one comin', with Iron Dave."

"He'll be killed."

"Him? Don't you bet on it, ma'am. He's all man, that one. I seen the way he treated Sproul. Like dirt, ma'am

First man I ever did see who worried Sproul. Worried him—yes, ma'am, he did."

"You'll not get me a horse, then?"

"I'm sorry, ma'am. Any other time."

Abruptly, she turned and walked quickly away.

Teale grinned. "Look at her go. She's mad all through."

"She'd have stopped the fight," Lahey said.

"Maybe, but I think she'd have watched it. That there's a game woman, you take it from me." He looked after her. "Lahey, we got to watch out for her. I'll lay you three to one she gets over there."

"You think I'm a fool, to take a bet like that? I'll lay you five to one she does, although I've got no idea how."

Suddenly Mary Tall Singer was walking beside Betty. "You want to go, I go with you," she said.

"I can't let you, Mary. There are bad men over there."

The Indian girl looked at her, her black eyes ironic. "You think maybe? I go . . . I have buckboard."

Barney Kilrone arrived in the vicinity of Hog Town just after daylight, but he did not go near the post or the town. He was dead-tired and he had a job to do. Finding a hidden dell near the river, he picketed the gray horse on some good grass, then bathed in the river. When the sun had dried him off he dressed, and then carefully checked out his gun. He had no proper cleaning materials, but he could wipe the gun free of dust and burned powder. He tore off a piece of his shirt and ran it through the barrel with a small twig; then he re-loaded the gun, wiping off each cartridge before loading.

When his gun was ready he led his horse to water, picketed it on fresh grass, and in the shade of a tree he lay down.

The outburst of gunfire from the post awakened him. He listened, gathering from the firing about what was happening. Then he went back to sleep. It was not likely that any Indians would come near Hog Town, and equally unlikely that the denizens of Hog Town would be out attracting attention to themselves. The gray horse was as good a sentinel as one could want.

Kilrone slept through the morning and into the afternoon and woke up hungry, which was what he had expected. He gave the gray horse another drink and had one himself. He had a bit of jerked beef in his saddlebags and he chewed on that. He wanted an empty stomach when he met Iron Dave. A man's wind is better with an empty stomach and he takes a punch better; and unless he had vastly overrated Iron Dave, he knew that he was going to take some brutal punches from Sproul.

He knew what he had to do. He had to break Sproul once and for all. He had to whip him, and whip him thoroughly, to remove the fear that many felt for him. Once Sproul had been whipped, he could never again command the same authority, for it was upon his physical strength and iron-hard fists that he based his control.

"You're a damn' fool," he told himself. "Who ever told you you could whip him?"

He did not know whether he could or not; he only knew that he had to try, and that he would never be satisfied until he had.

He saddled the gray, chewed on the jerky, and considered the situation before him.

He had to get into town and he had to find Sproul. He had to challenge him in such a way that he dared use no help, for Kilrone himself would have none. He had purposely avoided the post, knowing that there were some there who might wish to come with him, but he preferred not to involve anyone else.

He considered his own condition. He had not boxed in a long time, but he was in good shape. Sproul had come off the New York streets, had known street-fighting days in politics—he would know all the tricks of dirty fighting. As for himself, he had served his time at that sort of fighting, too, in the years of his knocking about.

There was no shooting from the direction of the post. Everything seemed to have quieted down there. Several times he went to the edge of the trees and looked out, but he saw no Indians anywhere.

Finally, when it was almost sundown, he heard a sound of activity from the post—some hammering, the crash of something falling. Evidently they had already started demolishing some of the half-burned structures in preparation for rebuilding.

He mounted his horse then and started toward Hog Town. At the outskirts of the tiny settlement he waited, studying the layout again, and then rode in, keeping himself out of view from all but a couple of windows. He came into the town's street, a street no more than a hundred and fifty yards long.

Behind him he heard movement and turned in his saddle. Teale was there, and with him McCracken, Lahey, Reinhardt, and half a dozen men he did not know.

"You boys looking for something?" Kilrone said.

Teale grinned at him. "Now, you didn't expect us to miss the best fight in years, did you? We figured to see the show and sort of pick a few fights ourselves if anybody elected to interfere."

"Thanks," Kilrone said. "Let's go inside."

His mouth was dry as he went up the steps and pushed through the door.

The big room was almost empty. The bartender stood behind the bar, and there were a few other men around, one of them with a bandage on his head. More than likely it was a memento of the night they came after the wagon. Iron Dave Sproul himself stood at the end of the bar, a big man in shirt sleeves and wearing a vest, with a massive chain of gold nuggets draped across the front. The vest was plaid, the shirt white, his trousers black and somewhat baggy-looking, as was the fashion.

Sproul took the cigar from his mouth and dusted the ash from it, then spat into the brass cuspidor. He threw a hard look at the soldiers who slowly moved around the room.

"Poole didn't make it, Dave," Kilrone said. "He was too good a man to work for you."

"I don't know anything about him."

"No? He told a different story."

Anger was rising in Sproul. This man had thwarted him, wrecked his plans. The destruction of the army post and its cavalry had failed. No telling where Medicine Dog was . . . if he was even alive. In any event, the moment was past. He would never be able to pull it off again . . . not here, at least.

"What do you want?" he said finally.

Kilrone was suddenly amused, and eager. It was coming up in him now, the old driving urge to destroy. He had built up a long antagonism for this man, and there was a time to end it . . . now.

"I came to whip you, Dave. I've heard about all that iron. Is it really there? Or are you a fraud?"

Sproul put down his cigar, placing it carefully on the edge of the counter. "Don't move that," he said to the bartender. "I'll want to finish it in a moment."

Kilrone unbelted his gun and handed it to McCracken, who was nearest to him. Sproul placed his on the bar and turned casually as if to face Kilrone, and then struck out viciously.

Kilrone, starting to turn, caught the blow on the corner of the jaw and it slammed him to the floor. He hit hard and skidded, his head bursting with lights. He heard the pound of boots as Sproul came at him and he rolled over, braced himself when he saw the man was too near, and dove at his knees.

Sproul side-stepped and laughed, kicking at Kilrone's head. The boot just scraped his skull, and then Kilrone lunged at the leg that was still on the floor. Sproul staggered, but caught his balance. Kilrone came up fast, went under a left hand, and hooked both fists into the mid-section. He smashed the second punch home with his left and then threw a high overhand right that caught Sproul on the cheekbone and staggered him, drawing blood.

They circled warily, Kilrone's head still buzzing from the first punch, a blow that by all rights should have finished him off. The iron was there, all right, in Dave Sproul's fists. He had never doubted that it was, knowing so much about the man, and had used the term only to taunt him.

Kilrone was being careful. He wanted desperately to win, to whip Sproul decisively, to beat him at his own game of knuckle and skull, but he dared take no chances. He not only had to guard himself against Sproul's attack, but against his own eagerness. His tendency was to wade in throwing punches, but a man would be a fool to trade punches with Sproul.

Sproul feinted and Kilrone started to step in. Sproul threw his punch and Kilrone dropped under the blow, and whipped a wicked punch to the mid-section. Sproul grunted, then came on. He struck Kilrone in the chest, staggered him, and then clubbed him brutally in the ribs and kidneys.

Kilrone crowded in, trying to trip the bigger man, but Sproul was used to that and braced his powerful legs. Kilrone found himself flung off balance and staggering against the bar. Sproul's eyes were gleaming with blood lust now. He came in, smashing a blow to Kilrone's ear that made his head ring; then he put a hook into his mid-section that almost lifted his feet from the floor.

Kilrone felt himself falling; but Sproul, suddenly sure of victory, caught Kilrone's shirt front in his left hand and shoved him back against the bar, drawing his right back for a finishing blow. Kilrone threw his right arm over Sproul's left and grasped the top of his vest, jerking him forward, and at the same instant Kilrone dropped his head and butted Sproul in the face with the top of his skull.

Sproul staggered back, his lips smashed and his nose streaming blood. With an inarticulate curse, he rushed, swinging with both big fists. There was no chance to side-step, no chance to evade. Kilrone lunged to meet Sproul and, dropping his head against the bigger man's chest, he began battering at his body with both fists. Sproul pushed him away, smashed a left to Kilrone's head and then a right, and as Kilrone tried to get inside the next punch, Sproul half turned and kicked him in the ribs.

A knife of pain stabbed at Kilrone's side and he gasped, his legs suddenly weak, and started to fall. Sproul kicked again at Kilrone's head; but in falling, Kilrone took the kick on the shoulder. He hit the floor on his hands and knees and scrambled forward, trying to grab Sproul's legs, but the big man skipped easily out of the way, amazingly light on his feet. Then stepping in, Sproul swung his boot and kicked Kilrone in the side.

Kilrone tried to pull away and he missed the full force of the blow; he staggered up, caught a smashing right on the chin, but his own weakness saved him and he was falling away from the punch into a table. With his last strength, he swung the table into Sproul's path and stopped the big man long enough to get his feet braced under him.

Kilrone shook his head, half blind with pain and fury, and as Sproul closed in for the kill, he leaped forward, stepping in fast and stopping the rush with a straight left to the mouth. He missed with a right, but curled his arm around Sproul's head and, catching hold of his left arm, threw Sproul over his hip to the floor.

The big man hit heavily, but came up fast. Kilrone hit him on the chin with a right before he could straighten up, and Sproul went to his knees, diving forward to grab Kilrone's legs. But Kilrone drove up with his knee, which caught Iron Dave in the face, smashing his nose into a bloody pulp.

Sproul came up and they stood toe to toe then, trading punches. Kilrone was a little faster, landing just often enough to take some of the drive from the punches he was catching. Every time he drew a breath he felt a stabbing pain in his side, and he knew he had at least one broken rib—probably more.

Sproul, shrewd enough to know Kilrone had been hurt, swung a hard right at his injured side, but Kilrone caught the blow on his forearm, then drove his fist into Sproul's mouth. By this time Sproul's lips were shredded and bloody, his nose was bleeding, and he had a welt over one eye, but he had hardly slowed down and was still coming in.

Backing away, trying to get his wind, Kilrone side-stepped. Sproul caught up a chair in one hand and swung it at arm's length in a sweeping blow that barely missed, shattering against a pillar. He closed in, landed a left to Kilrone's face, then a right. He was still cool, still confident. The big man had learned his fighting in many a bloody brawl such as this. He swung and missed, and for an instant was bent far over, and Kilrone clubbed him with a hammer blow to the kidney.

Sproul grunted and almost went to his knees. He started to come up, and Kilrone moved and hit him again in the same spot. He rolled to one side, flinging out a hand. His fingers grasped at Kilrone's shirt and it ripped in his hand. He struck with a left and Kilrone crossed his right over it, splitting the skin over Sproul's eye.

Kilrone was crouching now, to ease the pain in his side. Sproul circled, his big fists poised. He struck and Kilrone turned his head to avoid the blow, bringing his leg around in a sweeping kick that caught Sproul behind the knee. He fell forward, caught himself on one hand; but before he could straighten, Kilrone smashed him with another hammer blow to the kidney.

Sproul grunted and went to his knees. Kilrone split his cheekbone with a blow, and when Sproul got to his feet he backed away, studying the big man. Kilrone was badly hurt, and he had no idea how much longer he could stay on his feet. His breath was coming in ragged gasps, sweat trickled in his eyes, and they stung with the salt. He moved in, feinting; Sproul struck with his left and Kilrone pushed the punch over with his right palm, and then uppercut hard to the belly with his left. Sproul backed off and Kilrone followed. It had to be quick.

He blinked his eyes against the sweat, and crowded after the big man. Suddenly Sproul pivoted on the ball of one foot and kicked out with the other, swinging the leg around in a sweeping arc. Sucking in his mid-section to avoid the kick, Kilrone grasped Sproul's ankle with both hands and swung from the shoulder with all his strength. Already swinging with the impetus of the kick,

Sproul plunged across the room when Kilrone let go, his head crashing into a chair. He fell, started to get up, but fell again.

Kilrone drew back, gasping, each breath a stab of pain. He backed off, watching the fallen man. Suddenly Sproul started to move. He pushed himself up, got his knees under him, and staggered to his feet.

There was no question of quitting now. Kilrone, unable to straighten up, moved in, one hand holding his injured side, the other fist cocked. Sproul got his hands up, but Kilrone moved in, set himself and hooked viciously to the head. Sproul struck out, but the blow missed. Kilrone swung again from the hip, and Sproul staggered and almost went down. Kilrone knew he had strength for one more ... just one more. This one had to be it.

He cocked his fist, set himself and let go, his whole side swinging with the leverage of the blow. It caught Sproul on the point of the chin and he turned halfway around and fell, out cold before he hit the floor.

Bloody and battered, his shirt only a few trailing ribbons, Kilrone crouched over him, his breath coming in great gasps. Sweat and blood were dripping down his face, and he blinked at the fallen man, and prayed he would not get up again.

There was scarcely a sound in the room but his own breathing. Slowly, he backed off a step, then went to his knees. He stayed there, staring down at Sproul. But Iron Dave neither stirred nor even seemed to breath.

Kilrone felt hands lifting him, and he allowed them to help him to his feet. As he turned away he caught a glimpse of a wild, bloody figure in the mirror, a face he no longer recognized. There was a great purplish welt over one eye a long cut on his cheekbone, lips puffed and swollen ... most of the punches he could not even remember.

He turned his head, seeing a hand on his arm, feeling an arm about his waist. It was Betty.

"How did you get here?" he managed to say.

"Let's go home," she said. "You need to see Uncle Cart."

"Not as much as he does," he said, the words muffled by his swollen lips.

The white sheets were immaculate, the room was sunfilled and bright. Barney Kilrone clasped his hands behind his head and stared toward the window, wondering what was happening outside, but not curious enough to get up and look. He simply felt tired—tired from the fighting, tired from the riding, tired from the sheer strain of thinking, planning, wondering if each decision was the best one.

His muscles were sore. His side was taped and bandaged until he felt as if he was in a straight jacket, and every time he spoke or tried to smile he found his lips were stiff.

Betty Considine came into the room. "Uncle Cart will be back in a little while. He wants to look you over again."

"I'm all right. Has anybody seen Dave Sproul?"

She shook her head. "The Empire is closed and shuttered. Sergeant Dunivant told me most of the people were gone. They just picked up and pulled out after Sproul took that beating from you."

She looked down at him. "What are you going to do now?"

He shrugged, and tried to smile. "Drift, I guess. What else is there to do?"

"You could go back into the Army. Or you could be an engineer. Frank Paddock told Uncle Cart that you were one of the best in your class at the Point."

"I won't do it lying here." He started to get up and felt a sharp twinge of pain.

Betty put her hands on her shoulders and pressed him back. "You stay there! You are in no condition—"

He was smiling. She flushed and quickly took her hands from his shoulders. "Uncle Cart said you were to stay in bed," she said primly.

"Ever been to California?" he asked.

"California?"

"It's a nice place for a honeymoon," he said.

Dave Sproul tiptoed across his saloon and peered through a crack in the shuttered window. The street was still . . . no horses, nothing.

He went back to his quarters, where he knelt and lifted a board in the floor; he could look down into an opening between two of the foundation blocks. He took two sacks of gold from the hole and stuffed them into his saddlebags.

After a last look around, he went to the door and looked across the yard toward the barn. Nothing stirred there.

They were all gone. Everybody was gone. He had been whipped and they had all turned tail and left him. But he knew it was not only that he had been beaten, but that they all knew an order had been issued for his arrest on the testimony of Mary Tall Singer. Selling guns to the Indians . . . They had other evidence, he supposed, and undoubtedly Kilrone would testify.

They could send him to prison. Dave Sproul faced the fact; he had never dodged reality, and reality in this case meant the law. Well, the West was a big country, and there was always a new name, a new place, and a new beginning.

He went out the back door, closed it softly, and went to the barn. His horse was already saddled, the pack horse loaded. He would ride east, avoid towns, and reach the railroad in Wyoming.

He was stiff and sore, his head throbbing with the heavy ache left from the fight, his face battered almost beyond recognition. He chuckled . . . anyone who saw him now would not recognize him.

The horses were ones he had never used before. There was every chance he would get away; and he had money banked with Wells Fargo, as well as that he carried with him.

He went along the East Fork trail, camped the first

night on Raven Creek, and at daybreak was well away on the route he had chosen, riding southeast. By nightfall he was hunting a camping spot along Wolf Creek.

He was safely away. By the time he got to the railroad he would have grown a beard, and within a month he would be back in business. To hell with them! They couldn't stop him. As for Kilrone ... the son-of-a-gun could hit, damn him ... One day Kilrone would be riding or sitting down to eat and he would get a bullet right between the eyes.

That Indian girl, too. No wonder she was always around, watching, listening, saying nothing much. He'd figured she'd been gone on him, and all the while she was gathering evidence. He'd have a bullet for her too.

Sproul was not a frontier man, or a wilderness man, and he did not have the instincts and had not developed the senses as a man accustomed to living in those far-out places does. He found his camping place now, built a fire, and put water on to boil for coffee.

Far up on the slope he caught a flash of sunlight on something—probably it was mica or some other mineral formation. He picketed his horses, and was walking back to the campfire when the bullet hit him.

It took him right between the shoulder blades and turned him halfway around. He fell heavily, but got his hands under himself and, blindly, like a stricken animal, dragged himself toward the fire.

Medicine Dog wanted horses. Horses were important to an Indian: they made him a big man among his people. And the lone man He had seen had two fine animals. The Dog came down off the slope, approached the camp warily, and saw the man lying there, sprawled out. It was not until he turned him over that he saw who it was he had shot.

The Dog gave a grim chuckle. It was an odd thing that this should be the man he had killed. He was tugging the watch chain from Sproul's vest when Sproul opened his eyes. "Dog!" he said. "I—"

Medicine Dog ignored him, and ripped the nugget chain and the watch from the vest. Sproul was wearing a gunbelt, so the Dog pulled that off too. Sproul tried to sit up, and the Dog calmly smashed him on the skull with the butt of his rifle and continued his looting.

When he had gathered all he wanted, the Dog dumped some coffee into the boiling water and after a while he drank some. He glanced toward the white man—he felt nothing toward him at all.

After some time he mounted one of the horses and, leading the other, was about to leave. But he paused beside the body of Dave Sproul. Holding his Winchester in one hand, he pointed the muzzle at the fallen man and shot him again. Then he rode away, returning to the horses he had left in the hills.

The remains of the coffee boiled away, the coffee grounds burned, and the fire died out. Once, when only a few coals were left, the man moved slightly, then lay still.